Kidnapping Mr. Tubbs

BY THE SAME AUTHOR

Me, Cholay & Co.—Apache Warriors

Kidnapping Mr. Tubbs

by Don Schellie

Four Winds Press   New York

For reprint permission, grateful acknowledgment is made to The University of Illinois Press for "Make Me a Cowboy Again" from *The Hell-Bound Train: A Cowboy Songbook*, compiled by Glenn Ohrlin, copyright © 1973 by The University of Illinois Press.

LIBRARY OF CONGRESS CATALOGING IN PUBLICATION DATA

Schellie, Don.
  Kidnapping Mr. Tubbs.

  SUMMARY: Two teenagers sneak a very elderly ex-cowboy
out of his rest home for a visit to the ranch where he
spent his life. Their trip is full of unusual adventures
and Mr. Tubbs proves a surprising traveling companion.
  [1. Old age—Fiction.   2. Arizona—Fiction]
I. Title.
PZ7.S3433Ki   [Fic]   78-6153
ISBN 0-590-07542-X

Published by Four Winds Press
A division of Scholastic Magazines, Inc., New York, N.Y.
Copyright © 1978 by Don Schellie
All rights reserved
Printed in the United States of America
Library of Congress Catalog Card Number: 78-6153

1 2 3 4 5 82 81 80 79 78

Backward, turn backward, O Time, with your wheels,
Aeroplanes, wagons, and automobiles.
Dress me once more in sombrero that flaps,
Spurs and a flannel shirt, slicker and chaps,
Put a six-shooter or two in my hand.
Show me the yearlin' to rope and to brand.
Out where the sagebrush is dusty and gray
Make me a cowboy again for a day.

—''Make Me a Cowboy Again''

Kidnapping Mr. Tubbs

1

A. J. Zander didn't like it at all. Not anything about it. By nature he was a worrier, and right then he had plenty to worry about. His heart was beating like the bass drum at a football game, and the more he thought about what was happening, the more he worried and the faster and louder the drum-thumping became.

"Go on!" she whispered, giving him a push.

"Okay!" he whispered back. "Just quit shoving and be quiet. I'm listening." Hard as he listened, all he heard was the drum-thump of his heart. Or maybe it was hers. No, it wouldn't be hers. Eloise Ann Spencer had nerves of steel.

There were floodlights outside the place, but right there, right at the side entrance, it was dark and shadowy. His fingers gripped the handle of the heavy door, but before pulling it open he glanced once more around the parking lot. Still quiet. He had hoped that maybe someone might come along so they'd have to call it off, or at least postpone it. He wasn't that lucky.

At sixteen, A. J. had supposed he'd become rich and famous some day, but here he was, embarking on a career in crime. Already it was auto theft, if the police wanted to stretch the point. Now it was about to become breaking-and-entering, and in a few minutes it would be kidnapping and then flight to avoid prosecution. He watched a lot of television, so he knew law. They'd throw the book at him! He imagined his pictures, front view and profile, on one of those Wanted flyers in the post office lobby.

"Wanted for Kidnapping," it would say. "A. J. Zander, alias Alfie Boy." His Aunt Erna always called him Alfie Boy and he hated it. "Six feet, one-hundred-fifty pounds, dark brown hair, blue eyes, cute smile, pimple on side of nose. Armed and dangerous." The fingertips of his free hand explored his face. The left side—it was better. He hoped the FBI would find a picture of his left profile because he liked it better than the right one. Probably his mother had one; she had all kinds of pictures of him. She could open a gallery with just his baby pictures alone. It's a wonder she hadn't.

"Quit scratching your face and open that door!" Eloise whispered. "Somebody's going to see us out here!"

"I'm not scratching, and besides, sooner out here than in there," he said over his shoulder. "Out here it's prowling and that's just a misdemeanor. Inside it's burglary. That's a felony."

A felony. As he spoke the word he shuddered. She had made it all sound so simple and so logical and so innocent,

and like a very humanitarian thing to do. Why, she almost had him feeling like Albert Schweitzer or somebody over in Africa, but when you got right down to it, there wasn't much you *could* call it but a felony. Maybe though, since the "victim" was willing—was in on it, really—they'd go easy on them. Probation, even. No judge would ever send Albert Schweitzer to jail.

A. J. clenched his teeth and let out a breath. What was he doing here and why was he doing it, he asked himself, and then he shook his head, because he didn't know the answers. It just didn't make sense.

What did Eloise Ann Spencer mean to him, anyway? She was just a girl. Not that he didn't like her, because he liked her all right, but as a friend—a new friend, at that—and nothing more. She was older, going on eighteen, and she'd be graduating in June and going away to college and in two weeks she'd forget she ever even knew that tall skinny kid with the pimple on his nose. So it wasn't as if they were madly in love or even going together, or anything serious like that. Maybe in time it might turn into something serious—who knows about such things?—but for now, just being friends was enough. Too much. If he had the brains of a science-class lab mouse he'd break off that friendship right then and there, before he opened the door and it *was* a felony. Besides, she was fat. Well, maybe not *fat*, but she could stand to drop a few pounds, and then there were the braces. They sure didn't add a whole lot to her looks. And old. She was *so* old. What did he see in her, anyway? A. J. backed a few steps away from the door.

"It's all off," he said to her. "Forget it. At least as far as I'm concerned, forget it."

"A. J. Zander—you're a chicken! An absolute chicken!"

"I'm not chicken," the boy bristled. "You call it self-preservation."

"You promised . . ."

"Sure, I promised. I thought it would be fun. All of a sudden, though, it's not fun at all. I'm scared."

"Of what?" she asked.

"Getting caught."

"Even if we do get caught, what can they do to us? It's not like we're committing a crime, or something. We're not stealing anything."

"We're stealing the old man. Kidnapping, they call it. You can get life for kidnapping," A. J. said. "It's a federal offense." You'd never catch Albert Schweitzer kidnapping somebody, he thought.

"But Mr. Tubbs—he's *in* on this. He wants to take the trip. How can it be kidnapping if the victim is willing, and for that matter, if the victim isn't even a victim?" Eloise sighed. "Oh, A. J., you said you'd help. We need you."

"My folks need me, too. What's my mother going to say when she goes to the post office to buy a stamp and sees my picture on the wall? Why, she'd never write a letter again, I'll bet."

"You're being ridiculous! What we're doing is not a crime. We're just taking a sweet old man on a weekend trip. Nobody's going to go to jail for that!"

"You're sure? I mean, can you promise me?"

"Of course I'm sure," she said impatiently. "It's a kind, very humane act we're doing, and we'll be making a sweet old man very happy!"

The Albert Schweitzer business again. He sucked in a breath, then let it out slowly. There was just no arguing with her. She was in honor society and besides that, she was on the debate team. "Okay," he said. "You win, so let's get it done."

The door was heavy and A. J. drew it open slowly. Holding his breath, he listened. No alarm, not even a squeak of the hinges. That afternoon he had come here with Eloise and while she had talked with the nurse and held her atten-

tion, he had taped down the alarm button on the fire exit door and had taped the lock open. He'd seen it done on TV.

Along the corridor a few lights glowed dimly and at the end of the hallway, A. J. could see the brighter light of the nurses' station, which was located out of sight, just around the corner. He could hear low voices coming from there, and he could hear the muffled sounds of television beyond closed doors. For a moment they stood just inside the fire exit. "Should we crawl?" he asked Eloise.

"What on earth for?"

"I don't know—it just seems like a good idea."

"Well, if crawling gives you a thrill, go ahead. I'm walking." Slowly, quietly, they stepped down the corridor. The air was heavy with the aroma of dinner, mingled with smells of medicine and urine and disinfectant. It gagged the boy, just as it always did when he stepped inside the rest home.

A. J. hated the place. It bothered him. There were always so many old people around, and they made him nervous. You'd think that as many Saturday mornings as he had spent there, he'd be used to it by now, but it didn't work that way. It was bothering him as much now as it had the first time he had gone to visit his grandfather.

It was old Mrs. Koplin again, he realized. Though he tried not to think about her, she was always there in the shadows at the edge of his memory, all gray and hazy, her loving arms ready to reach out and hold him. But she had disappointed him, tricked him, so he tried not to think about her, but it didn't always work. Mrs. Koplin was every old woman he saw, and sometimes she was the old men too, except of course for Gramps. Gramps was Gramps. In some ways even Mr. Tubbs reminded him of the vague image of Mrs. Koplin that he carried in his mind. And here at the nursing home Mrs. Koplin was everywhere he looked.

The lounge was always the worst. Usually he tried to not

go in there, or if he did, he'd walk through quickly, careful to keep his eyes on his feet and not let them wander to the old people, who seemed to be everywhere. That afternoon he had had to go into the lounge and he had seen more old people at one time than he ever wanted to see again. They were just sitting, many of them staring off into space. A few talked among themselves, but mostly they simply sat doing nothing. One white-haired woman in a wheelchair was slumped over a bed pillow that was on her lap, her arms wrapped around it. She was sound asleep with her mouth open; canvas straps kept her from falling out of the wheelchair. Another woman talked to a rag doll as if it were a real baby, and patted its back and sang a lullaby to it. Near her two women were knitting or crocheting—A. J. wasn't sure which—and one man dozed, an open magazine on his lap. A television set was turned on to a game show, but nobody seemed to be watching it. They all were Mrs. Koplin. He kept remembering how they looked, especially that old lady with the doll, as he and Eloise moved slowly, quietly, along the nighttime corridor, keeping close to the wall.

"Help! Help! Help!" It was a woman's cry and it rose sharply above the television sounds. The voices coming from the nurses' station abruptly stopped. A. J. froze, pressing even closer to the wall. Again his heart was beating fast and his legs trembled. "They've heard us!" he whispered to the girl. "Now what do we do?"

"Inside the room," she said softly, pushing him into the third room on the left side of the hallway. His grandfather's room, Mr. Tubbs's room. She followed closely and when they were inside he leaned his weight against the closed door.

"Do we jump out the window?" he asked.

"No, A. J., we just go ahead as planned."

"But that cry for help ——"

"Forget it. You know as well as I do that that was just Mrs. Neeley. She's always calling out like that and the nurses mostly ignore her. Don't worry."

Don't worry—hah! A. J. Zander glanced about the room. It hadn't changed; it never did. The only light was the bluish glow of the television set and his grandfather's dim-burning bed lamp, which was tilted toward the pale green wall. Gramps was in his bed, just as he had been that afternoon, just as he always was, staring at the ceiling, motionless, with all those tubes going into him and coming out of him, keeping him alive. The boy walked to the bedside and placed a hand on his grandfather's shoulder, squeezing it gently. The old man's eyes looked up at him as if he were trying to say something. It must be awful, A. J. thought, not being able to move or to talk or to do anything. As he often had, he tried to imagine what it would be like, but he couldn't.

Mr. Tubbs was in his armchair, watching television. Homely old man Tubbs, A. J. thought. There just wasn't anything pretty about him. He had plenty of nose, and it was all covered with those tiny red veins old people get. The rest of his skin was wrinkly and loose and there were enough patches of stubbly gray whiskers on his chin and cheeks and neck to make A. J. wonder if maybe the old man had forgotten to put a blade in the razor when he shaved that morning. His eyes were watery and a sort of green, or maybe you'd call it hazel. It was hard to tell because he was always squinting, like a man who had spent his lifetime out of doors. He was bald as could be, but what hair Mr. Tubbs lacked on the top of his head, he made up for in bushy, bristly eyebrows. He almost needed hair spray to keep them in place. The old man was tall and had wide shoulders and huge hands that were all rough and scarred. When he walked, he walked tall and wasn't at all bent over, like so

many old people. Only now he wasn't walking. He was sitting in the chair watching television.

"He forgot," A. J. said to the girl. "Look at him—he's not even ready. He's in his bathrobe!" Eloise stepped forward and touched Mr. Tubbs on the shoulder. Turning, he looked up, a wide and toothless smile coming to his face.

"Shoot," he said, "you come! Didn't know if you'd turn up or not. Figured you might be funnin' me." He drew himself out of the chair and untied the belt at his waist and pulled off the bathrobe. Beneath it he was fully dressed; a washed-out plaid flannel shirt, a pair of faded Levi's, bedroom slippers. "It'll take me but a minute to get——"

The old man's voice was loud and Eloise quickly put her fingertips to his lips to quiet him, then raised a finger to her own lips. "Shhhhhh," she hushed, her face pinched in a frown. Mr. Tubbs smiled and nodded. He understood.

The old man was hard of hearing—"deef," he called it—and people had to raise their voices for him to hear. And like many people with hearing problems, his own voice was loud and it thundered through the whole wing of the rest home. So that afternoon when they were making their plans, the three had scribbled notes back and forth so they wouldn't be overheard. When their plotting was done, A. J. had carefully torn the notes to tiny bits and flushed them down the toilet. He had seen that on television, too.

"You got everything ready?" the boy whispered right into the old man's ear. Mr. Tubbs shook his head, shrugged, and pointed a finger at the ear. He hadn't heard. A. J. picked up the stub of chewed yellow pencil and pad of paper the old man kept handy and scribbled a note. Mr. Tubbs smiled, bobbed his head, and walked to the closet. Opening the door he bent over and picked up a rolled blanket secured with a length of fraying cord. He handed it to the girl, who tucked it beneath an arm. "And this," he said

to the boy, pointing to the floor of the closet. A. J. shushed him and looked to see what the old man was pointing to on the closet floor.

"A saddle!" he said, turning to Eloise. "Holy cow, he wants to take a saddle with him!" Shaking his head vigorously, he reached for the pad and pencil. "No saddle!" he scribbled. Mr. Tubbs read the note and dropped down into his chair.

"Ain't leavin' here without it!" he announced firmly. Hurrying to the table beside his grandfather's bed, A. J. scooped up the roll of adhesive tape from the supplies tray, ripped a few inches of tape from it, and plastered it over the old man's mouth.

"What on earth are you doing?" Eloise wanted to know.

"Him yelling like that—before you know it the nurses and orderlies and police and half the Marine Corps are going to come busting in here. If he has something to say, let him write it!" He handed the pencil and pad to Mr. Tubbs.

Thoughtfully the old man raised the pencil's tip to touch his tongue, but stopped short of his taped mouth. Frowning at A. J., he slowly wrote, "the sadel goze," underlining the words twice. A. J. had begun to write a reply when the sound of voices came from the hallway.

"They've heard us!" he said to the girl. "*Now* what do we do?" His face on that Wanted poster in the post office suddenly sharpened in his mind.

"Quick!" the boy said. "The window—it's our only chance!" Clutching the girl's hand he began pulling her across the room, but she resisted and shook her hand free of his grasp.

She wasn't moving.

2

"No, the closet!" Eloise insisted. "Into the closet! The window opens only a few inches!"

"That's the first place they'll look," A. J. said. "It's so obvious. In the spy pictures, everybody always hides in the closet!"

"But this isn't a spy picture," she argued, "it's real life. Besides, do you have any better ideas?" Glancing around quickly, the boy shrugged and shook his head. She was right; there was no other place to hide.

"So okay," he said. "Maybe the closet's *so* obvious nobody'll think to look in there." With the bedroll beneath her

arm the girl hurried across the room as A. J. quickly draped the bathrobe over the old man, who still sat in the chair, and tucked it around his shoulders. Then, yanking the tape from Mr. Tubbs's mouth, he sprinted for the closet and pulled the door shut behind him.

It wasn't an awfully big closet, and with the saddle on the floor, along with boots and shoes and the bedroll, there wasn't a lot of room for two people, too. It was cozy.

"I haven't hidden in a closet since I was little and used to play hide-and-seek with my cousins," Eloise whispered.

"I don't think I ever hid in a closet before in my life," said A. J. "Especially not with a girl." He shifted uncomfortably.

"Well, now you can say you have."

"Big deal." For a few seconds they were silent, then A. J. Zander sniffed. "Somebody or something in here smells like a horse," he said. "I'm going to sneeze."

"Don't you dare!"

"But I'm allergic!" He sucked in his breath sharply, building toward a sneeze. Suddenly Eloise pinched his nose. Hard.

"Whad ah you doey?" It hurt and A. J. was indignant.

"Quiet! I'm keeping you from sneezing."

"Lecko—iss padst!"

"You're sure?"

"I'b sure." Eloise released her hold and A. J. sniffled once more. "Don't you *ever* hold my nose again!" he said to her. "I don't like *any*one holding my nose."

"I had to keep you from sneezing."

"I could have done it myself, Eloise," he said. "I'm big enough to hold my own nose." He paused, then said, "Eloise."

"Yes?"

"Nothing, just *Eloise*. What a dumb name. It sounds like

somebody's old maid aunt." He sniffed again. "I'm going to call you Spence."

"I don't care what you call me, just don't sneeze!"

"Okay, then, Spence it is. That's better." She shushed him. Someone had entered the room.

"Oh, Mr. Tubbs, we're up late tonight, aren't we?" said a loud, female voice beyond the closet door.

"Ain't a whole lot after seven o'clock," the old man answered.

"Well, we'd better be thinking about bed soon," said the female voice. "You sleep well now, hear?" And then there was only the sound of television.

Cautiously, A. J. pushed the closet door open a crack and peeked out. The owner of the loud female voice was gone. "All clear," he whispered, and he crawled from the closet.

As he stood, Eloise—Spence—put out her hand and touched the boy's arm. "Don't get upset, A. J., but I think we'd better take the saddle."

"Why, he can't ride a horse—not at his age."

"I know it, but it seems awfully important to him. We'd better take it," the girl said.

The saddle. It didn't make any sense, taking it, but then none of this did. It was stupid, foolish, idiotic, dumb, and there was no way it could have a happy ending. He sighed. "Okay," he said, "so we take the saddle." Hauling it out of the closet, he pointed to it and nodded his head. Mr. Tubbs's face brightened. Hopping up from the chair, he threw the bathrobe over the foot of his bed and hurried to the closet.

The old man reached up to the shelf and brought down a beat-up old cowboy hat that was dirty and stained. He dropped it onto his bald head and grinned.

Eloise jabbed a finger at her wristwatch and Mr. Tubbs

understood. As they watched, the old man pulled on a Levi's jacket and buttoned it, fingered the wide brim of his hat, then picked up a pair of old, but carefully-shined cowboy boots from the floor. He looked to the boy and girl and nodded. "Reckon I'm as ready as ever I'll be," he said in that loud voice of his, and A. J. cringed. They could hear him six blocks away!

The boy picked up the saddle and started for the door, then stopped and turned. Stepping to the edge of his grandfather's bed, he lowered the saddle to the floor and leaned over and kissed his grandfather's cheek. "See you, Gramps," he said softly. Embarrassed then, he looked to see if the girl was watching. She wasn't and he was glad. He patted his grandfather's shoulder and then hauled up the saddle once more. "Let's get on the road," he said. "We've got a long drive ahead of us up to that ranch."

"I'll check the hallway," Spence said, "and then I'll go first. Mr. Tubbs can follow me and you bring up the rear."

"With the saddle," A. J. said sarcastically.

"With the saddle."

The way was clear and A. J. watched as the girl stepped into the corridor and headed quietly toward the fire exit. Under one arm she carried the bedroll and with her free hand she grasped one of the old man's hands. In his other hand, Mr. Tubbs held his boots. A. J. Zander had never carried a saddle before and it was heavier than he had expected it would be. He got a better hold on it and with both arms wrapped around it, he stepped out into the hallway, following the old man as closely as he could.

"Help! Help! Help!" cried Mrs. Neeley. A. J. froze, his heart skipping a beat. Two, maybe. Looking back over his shoulder he could see that the cry had brought no response. Poor Mrs. Neeley. He shuddered. Spence held the door

open for him and he crouched and ran the last dozen feet to the door and then outside into the cool April evening.

It was the saddle that did it, he supposed, because usually he didn't carry saddles and usually he was fairly sure of foot. Now, for the first time in his life he was carrying a saddle and he tripped. The momentum of that short dash carried him outside and across the narrow porch. On the single step his foot became entangled in a dragging stirrup—if that's what they were called—and sent him flying, head-over-heels-and-saddle, sprawling flat on his frontside in the pea gravel of the parking lot. A. J. Zander opened his mouth to holler in pain, thought better of it, and swallowed the yelp and his pride.

"You all right?" Spence asked, dropping to her knees beside him.

"I've been better," he answered, rolling over and sitting up. His palms burned from scraping along the gravel and his knees stung even worse.

"Anything broke, sonny?" It was the old man, bending over him. The boy shook his head. "Least nothing feels broke," he said. He was almost sorry. A broken leg or arm would've been a great excuse for him to pull out right then. "I think I skinned my knee, though," he added.

"Your knee?" Spence sniggered.

"What's so funny?" he demanded.

"Skinned knees are for kids. I used to have big scabs on my knees all the time when I was six or seven, but—well, never mind. If nothing's broken, we'd better get going. Can you make it to the car without help?"

"Of course I can!" There was an indignant tone in his voice. Slowly he stood, then looked down at the saddle. "See, I told you we shouldn't take it. We haven't even made it to the car and already it's causing problems!" He

kicked the saddle, then picked it up. A. J. hadn't limped more than a half dozen steps toward the car when he stopped again, dropping the saddle to the ground.

"My contact!" he said. "I lost my left contact!" He blinked his eyes, as if to underline what he had said.

"Do you need it?" asked the girl.

"Of course I need it," he said impatiently. "Do you think I'd wear contacts if I didn't need them?" Carefully he eased himself to his hurt knees and began looking for the lens.

"What's he lost?" Mr. Tubbs asked Spence.

"Contact lens," she said in his ear.

"What's that?"

"It's like glasses, like eyeglasses. They help you see better."

"He weren't wearin' none."

"He was, only you can't see contact lenses because they're real tiny and they fit over just the center of the eye."

"Shoot," said the old man, shaking his head as if he didn't believe her.

"A. J., you'll just have to make do without it. We can't take the time to look for it now, and besides, you'd never find it there. Not in all that gravel."

"But I'm blind as a bat without it," he argued.

"You still have the other one, don't you?"

"Sure, but——"

"So keep the eye without the contact closed and you'll be all right."

"You can do that for a little while, but not for long. It just doesn't work." He brightened. "So I guess you won't be needing me, after all. What good is a driver who can't see beyond the steering wheel?" He laughed. She didn't.

"A. J. Zander, you're coming along. We're in this

together and I can't manage without you. You don't have to drive—just help me take care of Mr. Tubbs." There wasn't any arguing with that tone in her voice.

Well, at least he had tried. In the parking lot there were four cars. He lived just a few blocks from the rest home, so he had walked. Eloise had driven. "Which car's yours?" he asked.

"The white VW."

"*VW?* We're going all the way up to Flagstaff in a Volkswagen? I mean, the three of us and the saddle?" As he neared the car he closed his eye without the contact and studied the car. "That thing belongs in a museum," he told the girl. "It looks like a relic. Why, it must be ten years old!"

"Older," she snapped, "and you hush up, A. J. You're not making things any easier." Spence reached the car first and opened the door on the passenger side. "Come on, baby," she said into the dark auto. "Be a good girl and jump out, now."

"Who's inside that car?" the boy demanded.

"Gwendolyn," she said, as if that explained everything. As she talked, a dog jumped gingerly from the front seat to the ground, its tail wagging, its body wriggling. "Good girl," said Eloise, bending over to scratch the dog behind its ears.

"I don't believe this!" A. J. said. "I really don't. I mean, here we are, a couple of hotshot kidnappers, and you bring a *dog* along in the getaway car!" He dropped the saddle for emphasis.

"Don't be so dramatic—it's not a kidnapping and the VW isn't a getaway car," said Eloise Ann Spencer. "And she's not *just* a dog—she's Gwendolyn!"

A. J. laughed and the dog or *the* Gwendolyn or whatever

it was, wriggled up to A. J., sniffed at him, then wriggled over to the old man and began sniffing.

"What kind of critter is that?" asked Mr. Tubbs.

"That's Gwendolyn," said Spence. "She's a basset hound."

"A basket what?"

"Hound," the girl said, speaking into the old man's ear. "A *basset* hound."

"Never seen such a foolish lookin' animal in all my life," said Mr. Tubbs. "All ears and feet and waggin' tail. What's she good for?"

A. J. didn't give Spence a chance to reply. "What made you bring the pooch?" he asked her. "And the Volks—why the Volks?"

"My parents are out of town," she said in answer to both questions. "No way could I leave Gwendolyn home alone or with somebody else. She'd miss me too much. But don't worry, she won't be any bother."

"If we're fixin' to go anyplace this evenin', we'd best be on our way before them nurses start checkin'," Mr. Tubbs said.

"That's the first sensible thing anybody's said tonight," A. J. agreed. "Open the trunk."

"What for?" asked the girl.

"This stupid saddle."

"Too big," she said. "Back seat."

"And the three of us in front?"

"Don't be silly. You know better than that," the girl said. "Only room for two in front—Mr. Tubbs and the driver."

"But you know I can't drive without my contact," he argued.

"Guess that puts you in the back seat then."

"With the saddle?"

She nodded. "There's only one problem. This car has a stick shift—on the floor—and I can't drive a car with a stick shift. I learned on an automatic."

"Then why didn't you bring the automatic?"

"My folks took the station wagon—*it* has the automatic transmission—over to California."

"So how'd you drive over here?" A. J. asked.

"It was parked in second gear so I drove over in second."

"The whole way?"

"It's only a couple of miles," she said, "and luckily I didn't have to back up or anything."

A. J. Zander couldn't think of anything to say, so he shook his head, pulled the seat forward, and wrestled the saddle into the rear, then squeezed himself in after it. "Sure not much room in the back seat of a VW," he grumbled, as he settled himself. "'Specially if you share it with a saddle."

Spence tossed the bedroll to A. J., who put it in the compartment behind the rear seat. Then she helped the old man into the front seat and he put his boots on the floor in front of him. "Hope you like dogs, Mr. Tubbs," she said to him, her lips close to his ear, "Because I'm afraid you're going to have to hold Gwendolyn."

"Never put much store in dogs, 'cept them what work to earn their keep, but if I got to, I got to. Hand 'im up here," he said, reaching for the animal.

"*Her*," Eloise said. "Gwendolyn is a her. And you don't 'got to,' Mr. Tubbs. A. J. can hold her in the back seat."

"He's *got to!*" the boy said. "No way that fat hound's coming back here. Bad enough to cuddle up with a saddle, but a fat, silly-looking dog like that, too? Not on your life!"

"She's not silly looking and she's not fat—she's well-nourished," Spence said, slamming the door on the

passenger side. Hurrying around the car she slipped in behind the wheel, turned the ignition key, and the engine sputtered to life. Then she flipped on the headlights.

"What do I do next?" she asked, looking back over her shoulder at A. J.

"You're really serious? I mean, you don't know how to drive this car, do you?"

"I said I didn't."

A. J. let out a deep breath. Women! "Okay, it's still in second?"

"Yes."

"Then put 'er in first and take off."

"Where's first?"

"Cripes. Just push in the clutch—that's the pedal on the left—and I'll shift for you." Stretching forward, A. J. reached over the seats and guided the stick into first gear.

"What now?" Eloise asked.

The boy glanced back toward the building. "Oh, great! The fire exit just opened and two people are hurrying this way—step on it!"

She did.

Spence gunned the engine a few times, then tromped the accelerator to the floor, at the same time lifting her other foot from the clutch pedal.

Jerking violently, the Volks shot forward, raising dust and spraying gravel. She wheeled sharply to avoid the tall bushes at the parking lot's edge and the auto spun in the loose gravel. Frantically she fought for control of the car, the heel of her hand striking the horn ring. The horn blared.

"Move your hand!" the boy cried from the rear seat.

"I did! Horn's stuck!" Surging forward, the auto set a snaking course across the lot. It missed the driveway by eight feet and bounced over the curb and onto the street.

Thrown against the saddle, A. J. loosed a yelp of pain and

the jolt over the curb knocked the old man's hat over his eyes.

"Good Lord, *I've been struck blind!*" shouted Mr. Tubbs as loud as he could.

Frightened, Gwendolyn suddenly lifted her muzzle and howled mournfully, deeply, the way bassets do.

"Driving a stick shift car is easier than I thought it would be," Eloise cried happily, as the getaway car, still in first gear, lurched crazily from the scene of the crime and zig-zagged into the night.

3

It was when they moved Mr. Tubbs into the room with Gramps, that it had all started. At least that's the way A. J. Zander had it figured, not that it mattered now. What did matter was that it had started at all. And as for Eloise Spencer, he had been seeing her around on Saturday mornings almost as long as his grandfather had been in the rest home, and that was a little more than a year. Until recently he had never talked to her, though.

Gramps had been living back in Minnesota when he had the stroke and when he was able to leave the hospital there, A. J.'s folks had flown back and brought him out to

Arizona. For several months he had lived with the Zanders, and the guest room had become a hospital room. But it was too difficult to give him the kind of care he really needed, and one Sunday A. J.'s mother had telephoned her brother and the two had agreed that Gramps should be in a nursing home. For days A. J.'s mother had cried about it, but she realized it would be best for everybody concerned. It was the practical thing to do.

A. J. had never gotten to know his grandfather as well as he would like to have known him, though some of his earliest memories—besides those of Mrs. Koplin—were of Gramps. Vaguely he could remember that when he was small and his family still lived in Minnesota, he used to spend Saturday mornings with his grandfather. In the summertime they would fish or they would go for long walks in the woods, and when winter came they would build things in Gramps' workshop, and if the ice were solid on the lake, they would go skating.

But then his family moved to Arizona and, except for a long-ago vacation to the Midwest and one Christmastime when Gramps flew out to spend the holidays with his family, A. J. hadn't seen his grandfather for years, until they brought him to the house in the ambulance. Then he didn't look at all like A. J. remembered him. He didn't even resemble the man who had taken him fishing.

After school the boy would go into the guest bedroom to be with him, but he never knew what to say to his grandfather, and besides, there was no way of knowing whether he understood or even heard anything, anyway, because he wasn't able to speak. So mostly A. J. talked about school and what he had done that day, and he'd practice aloud his verb conjugations for Spanish, and all the while Gramps just lay there, looking at the ceiling. Talking to Gramps was like trying to hold a conversation with the

mulberry tree in the front yard. Somehow, though, it made A. J. feel good and he hoped it made Gramps feel better, too, having him sit beside the bed.

Then Gramps went to the rest home and always on Saturday mornings A. J. would go to visit him. Saturdays were for Gramps again, just as they had been in Minnesota.

The room had two beds in it and over the months there had been a succession of four, or maybe it was five, sick old men occupying the second bed. A. J. never knew what happened to them. He would step into the room on a Saturday morning to visit and somebody different would be in the other bed. Once he asked a nurse what had happened to old Mr. Steele, who was the first one, and she smiled and shook her head and told him, "Oh, Mr. Steele is no longer with us," and the boy never knew whether he had moved to a different nursing home, had gone to live with family, or had died, or what. Died, A. J. supposed. After Mr. Steele, he never asked where the old men had disappeared to. He didn't want to know. Mr. Martinez followed Mr. Steele, and after Mr. Martinez, it was Mr. Huffman, and then there came Mr. Tubbs—there might've been someone else for a short time just before him—and Mr. Tubbs was different. He wasn't sick, just old.

With Mr. Tubbs around, A. J. never had to worry about what to say to his grandfather. Mr. Tubbs did all the talking. He had been a cowboy all his life and he had plenty of stories to tell about his life. Mostly A. J. enjoyed the stories, except when the cowboy began repeating them, yet it was much easier for A. J. than trying to think of something to say to his grandfather.

"Ever tell you, sonny, 'bout how me'n Seth got into trouble one time down to Prescott?" he asked one Saturday morning as he settled into his armchair. Before A. J. could say yes, that he'd heard the story, Mr. Tubbs had his mouth

going and the boy heard the story for the sixth, or maybe it was the seventh, time.

"Happened that things was slow up to the ranch and me'n Seth took us a few days off and rode down to Prescott to have us a time." The old man paused in the telling of the story and he smiled, a faraway look in his watery eyes, and he gave his head a slight shake.

"Well, we was hellin' round town lookin' for some mischief we could get into and we found us some, we did. Rode our horses plumb into the lobby of a fancy hotel, just to say we'd done it. Would've been no problem to speak of," he went on, "exceptin' some old lady from the East took to screamin' and spooked Seth's horse and that got mine to actin' up somethin' fierce and—well, we about made sawdust out of the furniture and rags out of them fancy carpets, and before we knowed it, me'n Seth was residin' in the pokey as special guests of the Town of Prescott. Disturbin' the Peace, they called it." Mr. Tubbs laughed. "Shoot, I reckon we *did* disturb it but good.

"Took us upwards of two years to do it, but we paid off the damages—couple hundred dollars, it was—down to the last penny. For a long time, though, me'n Seth wasn't hardly on speakin' terms with the law in Prescott. My, but we had us a time."

It sounded almost like something out of a Western movie—a bad one—and A. J. didn't know whether to believe it or not. That was the trouble with the old man's stories. The boy wondered how much was really true and how much was just his imagination.

"Whatever happened to your pal, Seth?" A. J. asked, just to be polite.

"You'll have to speak up, sonny," the old man said. "I'm a trifle deaf."

"Your friend Seth—whatever happened to him?" A. J. was almost shouting.

"He rode on, in time. Montana, it seems, or maybe Colorado. Makes no nevermind where. Most ever'body rode on after a spell, one place or another, cowfolks bein' mostly a restless lot. 'Cept me, perhaps—I stayed put. Like a wart on a nose, I stayed put till they had to root me out."

"You never wondered about what was beyond the next hill?" It was a female voice and A. J. quickly turned his head toward the door to see who it belonged to. It was that girl with reddish hair and braces he'd been seeing around the rest home.

Brightening, Mr. Tubbs rose from his chair. "Missy— how-do. Didn't hear you ride up." Ride up. A. J. winced. The girl hurried across the room and squeezed the old man's outstretched hand and then hugged him. He smiled and his false teeth slipped.

"How's my favorite cowboy?" she asked, and while Mr. Tubbs thought of an answer, she turned to A. J. and mouthed a quiet, "Hi." A. J. tried to smile and then mumbled an uneasy, "Hello."

"Well, how about it, Mr. Tubbs?" she said. "Didn't you ever wonder about what was beyond that next hill? I thought all cowboys did."

The old man lowered himself to his chair again and crossed his legs. "'Course I wondered," he said finally. "I kept imagining all likes of grand things over there. But I was contented where I was there at the Pfeffer ranch, and I figured, what if I left there and went lookin' for somethin' better and never found it? Why, I wouldn't have nothin' then, so I stayed put and done my job as best I could. Paid off, I reckon. Even in slim times when ridin' jobs was scarcer'n gold in a dollar watch, they kept me on the payroll."

"Weren't you ever sorry that you never found out what *was* beyond that next hill?"

For the better part of a minute the old man sat quietly, his

eyes studying his hands. A. J. wondered if he hadn't heard the question. Finally Mr. Tubbs gave his head a shake. "Nope," he answered. "Can't say that I've ever been truly sorry. It was purely my choice. Wasn't anybody made me stay there and, as I said, they treated me right, treated me fair, all them years, and well, that place—it got to be home for me. Only home I ever knowed since I was a tad."

"Well, *this* is your home now," the girl said with a sweep of her arm, "and you've got everything you'll ever want or ever need right here."

"She's right," said A. J., nodding. "Why, you've got it good right here."

"Shoot," said Mr. Tubbs. "Ain't nothin' here but walls to coop a man up and to keep the outside from gettin' in. Walls and bothersome ladies, forever fussin' over me like I was an orphan calf.

"Why, a man can't ride off and be by himself when he has a mind to. Can't sit his horse on the rise of a hill and watch the sun go down of a summer evenin'.

"Them mountains," he said quietly. "I miss seein' them mountains all about, 'stead of puny green walls, and I miss all that sky above, and the meadows with grasses belly-high to a cow. An' I miss kneelin' at a mountain crick to drink of the icy waters in the spring of the year. Shoot, I *do* miss that place."

"It sounds awfully pretty," the girl agreed.

"I keep thinkin' someday I'd like to go back up north for just one more look at all them things 'fore I die."

"Who knows, Mr. Tubbs?" the girl said cheerfully. "Maybe you will get back up there some time."

The old man laughed. "I know better'n that," he said. "My birthday is comin' up—reckon I must be near a hundred, best I figure it—and I know there ain't goin' to be many more birthdays after that'n. Fact, it'll likely be my last. Man gets as old as me, well . . . "

The old man lowered his chin, raised his bushy eye-brows, and gazed directly at the girl, as if to underscore what he had said.

"Don't talk that way, Mr. Tubbs," said the girl. "You're real healthy—you'll be around to blow out the candles on lots more birthday cakes."

"Ain't so, missy, and you know that well as I do. Nope, I've saw that ranch for the last time. The *very* last time."

A. J. caught the girl's glance. Her eyes looked peculiar, as if she were thinking awfully hard. Exactly what it was he saw in them, he didn't know, but whatever it was, he was sure he didn't like it. He turned away quickly, before her eyes met his.

4

"I'm Eloise Spencer," **the girl said to A. J. after a few** moments. "Here we've been talking like old friends and we don't even know each other. Not officially, at least."

A. J. hated introductions. He never knew what to say, so he settled for a weak, "Hi," then cleared his throat. "I'm A. J. Zander. The one in that bed—he's my grandfather."

"I thought he must be," said Eloise. "I see you here on Saturdays."

"Me too. I mean I see *you,* too. Do you work here?"

"Volunteer."

"You mean you come here with all these old people when you don't even *have* to?"

She nodded. "I like it, I really do. I like working with people."

"Even—old ones?"

"Even old ones," Eloise answered emphatically. "Maybe even *especially* old ones. They have a lot of problems and they need help. And they're so lonely—they love to have somebody visit them."

She walked to where Mr. Tubbs was sitting and raised her voice so he could hear. "And besides, you meet such interesting people here and make such good friends. Isn't that right, Mr. Tubbs?" Eloise patted his arm.

"Shoot," the old man said. He seemed embarrassed.

"So what do you do, empty bedpans?" A. J. wanted to know.

"I read to them and help with crafts and write letters for some of them, but mostly I just talk with them. I'm pretty good at talking, but I'm a good listener, too. They like to have somebody to talk to."

The thought of Mrs. Koplin came to the front of his mind again and A. J. shuddered. "If it wasn't for Gramps—my grandfather, I mean—I'd never even set foot in this place or any place like it. Just being here spooks me."

"That's silly. You don't like old people?"

He shrugged. "I guess that's it. They make me feel—oh, I don't know—peculiar, call it."

"But everybody gets old, eventually, A. J.," said the girl. "Even you will, if you're lucky."

"Not me," he said grinning. "I'm never going to get old. I'm going to find the Fountain of Youth that Spanish guy was looking for, and I'll be a teen-ager forever."

"Good luck," she said, glancing at her watch. "Oh-oh—I'm in trouble. I promised Mrs. Schultz I'd read to her today and she gets awfully upset if I'm late." And then Eloise was gone.

That had been three weeks ago. They had talked several more times and come to know one another better the next few Saturday mornings. Eloise was a bit peculiar—the old people, and all—but he liked her. She went to North Valley High School and would be graduating in June, and after that she planned to go to the university here in town, where her father was a professor of something. Sociology, A. J. thought. But every time they met and talked those Saturday mornings she would bring up the matter of poor old Mr. Tubbs, and wouldn't it be wonderful for him to see that ranch just one more time, and the boy would nod and say, "Sure," and then change the subject. She had something in mind—A. J. could feel it—and even though he wasn't sure what it was, he *was* sure he didn't like it. Then, last Saturday morning, he found out exactly what the girl had in mind and he had been right. He *didn't* like it.

It was at the soft-drink machine near the front entrance that they met. "Can I buy you a cola?" offered A. J.

"I don't drink them," she said. "My dermatologist says I shouldn't. Acne."

"I'm glad I don't go to *your* doctor," said the boy dropping a coin into the machine.

"Saturday," she said after he took a sip of the soda, "is Mr. Tubbs's birthday. Just think, a week from today he'll be one hundred years old."

"That's what he thinks. He says he's not really sure."

"Well, if it isn't his hundredth birthday, it's awfully close to it," Eloise Spencer said. "I think we ought to give him a surprise."

A. J. took a long drink. "Great," he said. "You bake a birthday cake and I'll buy him a pair of socks."

"That's not the kind of surprise I had in mind." Moving closer to A. J., she touched his arm. "Let's drive him up to the ranch! That would be the most wonderful thing we or anybody could possibly do for him!"

"He's so old—they'd never let him out of here," A. J. said.

"I know. I'd thought of that. We'd have to—well, sort of sneak him out."

"I like my idea better. A man can always use another pair of socks. They're always getting holes in the heels."

"Be serious, A. J. I mean it."

"But that would be kidnapping!"

"It wouldn't either, because Mr. Tubbs would be in on it with us. Anyway, we wouldn't be holding him for ransom, or anything like that. We'd just drive him up there and after he'd seen the place, bring him back. Why, they'd hardly miss him."

"Well, if it isn't kidnapping, it must be something that's against the law. I mean, you don't just come into a place like this and sneak out with some old guy."

"Just think of it as being a chance to help your fellow man," the girl said.

"He's not *my* fellow man. Why, he's nothing to me. A nice old guy, maybe, but a month ago I'd never even met him. I'd never even met you, either, for that matter."

"A. J., here you have a wonderful chance to do a great thing for a sweet old human being and you're going to blow it. Why, except for us, Mr. Tubbs has *no*body. No family, no real friends, even. We're all he has!"

"Okay, I can see that. I feel sorry for the guy, being all alone, but that doesn't mean I have to get that involved with him. What if we should drive him up there and he gets sick or even dies? We'd be responsible."

"You can't think of things like that. You could go all through life not doing anything because somebody might get sick or die. We'll just pick him up here Friday evening, right after his dinner, and we'll have him back Saturday night. I can't drive all that way myself, A. J., and keep an eye on him and everything. I need you to help me."

"Driving? You want me to do the driving?" Why hadn't she mentioned that earlier? He liked to drive, but borrowing a family car was next to impossible. When he went out with the family his father always drove, and when he was with his mother, *she* drove. A. J.'s driving made her nervous, she always said. Everything made her nervous.

"Sure, all of it if you'd like," Spence said. "I'm not all that wild about driving on trips. I like to look at the scenery."

The boy nibbled at his lip and frowned. "I don't know," he said, a note of doubt in his voice.

"I'll bet you're afraid to do it," she said. "Is it your parents? Is that what you're afraid of?"

"'Course not," A. J. snapped. But it *was* his folks. They'd be furious if he ever did anything like that. He'd never hear the end of it. "What about *your* Mom and Dad?"

"They wouldn't mind. Besides, they'll be out of town," she said. "They're going to a conference in San Diego."

"And they're leaving you alone?"

"With Gwendolyn."

"Who's Gwendolyn, your housekeeper?"

"Our dog. She has papers."

"Your folks are going out of town and just leaving you with the dog?" A. J. shook his head. "If my folks went out of town they'd probably hire a stupid baby-sitter for me!" Then he was sorry he'd said it.

"They must baby you a lot," she said softly.

A. J. shrugged it off. "And we'd be gone only from Friday night until Saturday night?" Only. That was the hitch. How would he ever explain to his parents where he had been from—*only*—Friday night to Saturday night? He sighed.

Making such a decision wasn't easy. Always his folks decided things for him. His mother even decided what clothes he'd wear to school the next day and laid them on

his bedroom chair the evening before. Sometimes he got to feeling like he was a stick floating in a river, just going along with the current. It was always much easier letting them decide things for him than it would have been for him to resist and make his own decisions.

"I don't know," he said, a pained expression on his face. "Really, I just don't know . . ."

"Why not, A. J.? If it's not your folks you're worried about, why not?"

"Because—because . . ." There were a million reasons *why not,* but he couldn't find words to tell her a single one. "Okay," the boy said weakly. "Okay—I'll do it."

Which is how A. J. Zander happened to be in that beat-up VW with a howling dog, an old cowboy in a big hat that kept slipping down over his eyes, a saddle, a wild woman driver at the wheel, and a horn that just wouldn't quit blowing.

"Pull in here and park," shouted A. J. from the rear seat. "We've got to get that horn stopped." It was a shopping center parking lot and, except for a dozen or fifteen cars in front of the supermarket at the far end of the lot, it was deserted.

Spence braked, then wheeled sharply off the street into the exit driveway. A. J. gripped the back of the front seat. His mother should drive with Spence. That would give her something to be nervous about.

"Where should I park?"

"Anywhere! Just pull up anywhere and turn off the motor." Spence jammed on the brakes and the white Volks stopped abruptly, almost throwing the old man and the dog through the windshield. The engine died. "You forgot to put in the clutch," he said to her. "Turn off the ignition."

"Where's the horn?" he asked her after they both left the car.

"On the steering wheel, of course."

"I don't mean that," he said impatiently. "I mean, is it up front in the trunk or in the back by the engine or——" He stopped mid-sentence as he noticed the police cruiser pulling up beside the Volkswagen.

And to think they hadn't even made it three blocks from the rest home. If only he'd been driving, at least the getaway would have been successful. Some caper! He wondered how much the bail would be for kidnapping.

5

The policeman inside the patrol car spoke something into his microphone, then slowly opened the door, not once removing his gaze from A. J. The boy shivered. He could almost feel those eyes on him and nervously he moved his hands toward his pockets to keep them from fidgeting, but thought better of the idea and crossed his arms over his chest. For a fleeting moment A. J. considered running, but then he saw the size of the thirty-eight holstered on the cop's equipment belt and decided to stay put. With a long, five-celled flashlight in his left hand and his right hand hanging not far from the butt of the thirty-eight, the policeman slowly approached them. It seemed to take forever.

As the officer drew closer he looked from A. J. to Spence and then back to A. J., shining the beam of his flashlight in the boy's eyes first, then hers, then his again. A. J. squinted and then the brightness went away as the officer walked past them and leaned over to shine the light into the car, on the old man, on the dog.

Apparently satisfied, the policeman seemed to relax, and turning back to the boy and girl, he spoke. "I'm Officer Barlow—you folks got troubles?"

"Only the horn," said Eloise, shouting to be heard above the blaring noise. "We were driving along and suddenly it just started blowing and it won't stop. Do you know how to turn it off?"

"Let me have a look," the policeman said. Walking to the front of the car he squatted and reached beneath the bumper. "Here," he said, handing A. J. the long flashlight. "Hold this for me." A. J. aimed the beam toward the front of the car, his hand still trembling. He hoped the cop wouldn't notice how nervous he was.

Almost as suddenly as it had started, the horn stopped blaring and the silence startled the boy. "That's got it," the policeman said, sounding proud of himself. "Better have a mechanic have a look at it and get it working." Once more then he glanced from the girl's face to the boy's, and then he flashed his light into the VW.

"You okay, mister?" he asked Mr. Tubbs. The old man was staring straight ahead and didn't turn to face the officer.

"He has a hearing problem," Spence explained.

The policeman nodded. "Everything else all right?" he asked.

"Just fine," the girl said. "It was just that horn. Thank you for fixing it."

"Sure," he said, and smiling, he turned, climbed into the patrol car, talked into the microphone again, and then pulled away.

A. J. let out a deep breath, then turned to Spence. "I thought that was the end of our little adventure right there," he said. "I figured he was going to run us right on down to juvenile."

"For having a stuck horn?"

"Don't be silly. I mean, I figured he was suspicious of us, and that they had a report about Mr. Tubbs being missing, and—well, forget it. I guess right now you'd better learn how to drive that car of yours. You sure can't expect to drive it all the way up to Flagstaff in first gear."

Eloise spoke to Mr. Tubbs and he got out of the car and sat on a planter in the parking lot. Then she snapped a leash on the dog and handed the loop to Mr. Tubbs. "Now, don't you two go 'way," she said to the old man. "We'll be back before you know it."

Spence sat behind the steering wheel and A. J. was in the seat beside her, and with his hand cupped over hers on the gearshift knob, they circled the parking lot. Stopping, starting, speeding up, slowing down. Round and round they drove. "When you change gears, you push in the clutch pedal," he told her. "That's your left foot. And then you let the clutch up slowly as you press down on the accelerator. That's your right foot. You use that foot for the brake pedal, too. The brake's the one between the clutch and the gas." From first to second to third to fourth, then back down to third, to second. Reverse, then. Back and forward and back again. "You're picking it up pretty fast," he told her as she pulled up in front of where Mr. Tubbs and Gwendolyn waited. "Before you know it you'll be handling this car like a pro."

"I hope so," she said. "It's a long way to Flagstaff." A. J. climbed into the rear seat. Mr. Tubbs slowly eased himself into the car and the dog leaped up, placing her large front paws on the old man's leg. Her rear legs, though, remained on the ground. Eloise called to the dog, urging her

to jump. Gwendolyn wouldn't. The girl got out of the car
and walked around to the passenger side.

"You're just getting so fat and lazy," she said to the
animal, "that we're going to have to put you on a diet."
Gwendolyn wagged her tail at the attention as Spence lifted
the dog's hind quarters onto Mr. Tubbs's lap. He "oofed"
under the dog's weight. Gwendolyn looked up and licked
him on the face and he wiped at the place with the back of
his hand. "Shoot," he said to the dog. "Let's not have none
of that!"

Behind the steering wheel again, Spence turned on the
ignition and flipped the starter. "Well," she said enthusiastically, "we're off!" The VW lurched forward a few feet
and the engine stalled.

"Try again," A. J. told her, "only this time put it in first.
You still had it in fourth gear." The girl shifted into first,
started the engine, eased up on the clutch, and pressed
down on the accelerator.

"Okay, so *this* time we're off," Spence said as the car
moved slowly and jerkily through the parking lot. "Which
way?"

"What do you mean, which way? I figured you'd know
all of that, like where we were going and how to get there
and all. Didn't you bring a map?" She shook her head.

"Don't you worry none," said Mr. Tubbs. "Sonny, hand
me my blanket roll. Got me a dandy map in there." A. J.
reached behind the seat, pulled out the rolled-up blanket,
and passed it over the front seat to the old man. Spence
stopped the auto, slipped the gearstick into neutral, and
pulled the emergency brake, letting the engine idle. Then
she turned on the dome light and helped the old man juggle
dog and bedroll. He slipped a hand inside, among the folds,
and appeared to fish about for a time, then withdrew the
map.

It was yellowed and brittle with age, and it was torn on the creases. Leaning forward for a better look, A. J. watched as Eloise unfolded the map. "Oh, for Pete's sake," he said, "that map's from the 1920s—it belongs in a museum!"

Eloise turned sharply toward the boy and frowned, then looked back at the map. "I'm afraid A. J.'s right, Mr. Tubbs," the girl said. "They've been building a lot of roads lately and I think we'd better find a map that's a little newer than this one."

"Never once failed to get me where I was goin'," Mr. Tubbs said. A. J. could see that the old man's feelings were hurt.

"Never mind what he says," A. J. whispered to her, "we can't take off with just *that* map. We'd get so lost nobody would ever find us!"

The old man grunted and stuffed the map back into the bedroll, and Eloise put the car in gear and drove out of the parking lot and onto the street, heading in the direction of the Interstate. "There's a gas station up ahead," she said. "They'll have a map."

"Good idea," said A. J. "We'd better gas up, anyway, before we hit the road. My dad always does. What's the gas gauge say?"

"It doesn't," she answered, steering into the filling station. "It hasn't worked for years. Usually my father is the only one who drives this car and he says he can sense when it needs gas."

"This is incredible," said A. J. shaking his head. "Nobody's going to believe me when I tell them about this. I mean, you couldn't make up a story like this. Kidnapping a 'deef' old cowboy—snatching him out of a rest home, of all things—and the getaway car is a beat-up old clunker with a busted gas gauge and busted God-knows-*what*-else, and

there's a fat, dumb old dog named Gwendolyn along for the ride, and a smelly old saddle in the back seat taking up so much room I can hardly move, and the wheelman never even drove a car in her life! Like I said, incredible!''

Spence parked the car beside a row of gasoline pumps, turned off the motor, and looked back at the boy. "It's not incredible," she said icily. "I've had a license since the day I turned sixteen, only I've always driven automatic, and Gwendolyn is *not* dumb! And—and—and—'' She climbed out of the car and slammed the door and headed for the ladies' room, and A. J. got out and leaned against the auto.

"Fill 'er up," he said as the attendant approached.

"Where's the bathroom?" called the old man from the car. A. J. pointed around the corner of the building, snapped the leash on the dog, and lifted her off Mr. Tubbs's lap. Then the old man climbed out and headed for the men's room. "Better check the oil and tires, too," the boy told the attendant, "and make sure the windshield's good and clean." And then he added, "We'll be on the road." A. J. ignored the attendant's curled lip as he led the dog inside the service station, where he helped himself to an Arizona road map from a rack on the wall.

As he returned to the car the attendant was leaning against a front fender, his arms crossed over his chest, his foot tapping on the concrete. "This gonna be cash or you want it on your credit card, sport?"

"Cash, I guess. But the girl—she's paying."

"Then *she's* the heavy spender, eh? Think she can handle it?"

"Why?" asked A. J. "Is it that much?"

"Yeah," the other said. "The tank took all of thirty-seven cents' worth. Most people use credit cards instead of carrying *that* much cash."

Wise guy, thought A. J. How was *he* supposed to know

how much gas was in the car, what with that stupid gauge being broken and all? "Never mind her," he said. "I'll pay—here, hold the dog." He handed the attendant Gwendolyn's leash and dug into his pocket. Her tail wagging, she sniffed at the filling station man and he eyed the dog suspiciously. "There you go," A. J. said, dropping the coins into the other's hand. "Even change, yet." The attendant put the money in the cash box and walked to the other island of pumps, where another auto had pulled up. The old man returned to the VW and then Eloise appeared, her wallet in hand.

"Never mind," A. J. told her, "it's taken care of. I paid the guy. After this, though, you're bankrolling the trip."

"But A. J., I think I should——"

"Never mind," he said, brushing his hand through the air. "I got it. Don't worry."

"Yeah, girlie," the attendant called, "the sport there—he already paid me. All thirty-seven cents of it!"

In cool silence A. J. climbed into the back seat, his ears burning. What business did that attendant have, horning in like that? He should have poked him in the nose. Maybe he should write a letter to the president of the oil company, instead. That would bring results. Still fuming, A. J. unfolded the map and studied it as Mr. Tubbs and Gwendolyn got settled. Spence started the car and looked back at A. J.

"Just go over to Grant Road and then turn left to the Interstate. You get on there and just stay on—that's all you have to worry about until we're way up beyond Phoenix."

It was early evening and the traffic was light. A. J. leaned forward, his arms resting on the backs of the front seats, and with one eye closed, watched the streets to make certain Spence got onto the Interstate with no problem. Now and again he glanced through the rear window, keeping an eye out—his good one—for police cars. A. J. had been sure

they'd be picked up by this time. In a way he was almost disappointed that they hadn't been. Now that he couldn't do the driving, the idea of the long trip didn't seem like such a kick, after all.

Steering the car up the entry ramp, the girl easily merged with the sparse traffic on the Interstate. Gwendolyn was curled up on the old man's lap, sound asleep, and Mr. Tubbs's head was nodding. "Which one's snoring?" A. J. asked. Spence didn't reply and A. J. sighed. "Probably both," he muttered, answering himself, and then he leaned back in the seat. "Guess I'll join 'em," he said.

He shifted in an attempt to get comfortable, but with that smelly old saddle taking up more than half the rear seat, comfort was out of the question. So instead of cozying down and sleeping, he sneezed and thought.

He thought about his folks. They had gone to a dinner party so it would be at least two or three more hours before they returned home and found the note he had left stuck to the refrigerator door with the magnet that was supposed to look like a stalk of celery. A. J. wondered about the note and he worried about it. Maybe he had said too much. Too little, maybe. He had thought about not leaving any note at all, but he had decided he'd better leave one because the Zanders were a note-leaving family. Sometimes he thought he communicated more with his mother and father with notes on the refrigerator door than in plain, eyeball-to-eyeball talking. His mother was always off to meetings or bridge games or luncheons or shopping and his father worked a lot of evenings. So he had left the note, hoping they'd understand. His mind traced the felt-tipped words:

"MOM—" it began. Most of his notes were to Mom. "I have left, but I will be home again soon. Maybe tomorrow. Don't worry. Is Mr. Katz still our lawyer?" And then he had signed it "Alfred."

His parents always got upset when he called himself A. J. or when his friends called him that or when he signed his notes to them with his initials, and right then was no time to upset them any more than necessary. Alfred. He was the only guy in his class—in the whole school, even—who was named Alfred. And Jacob, his middle name, was even worse. He had gone through asking his friends to call him Al and Alf and Alfie and Jake and had finally settled on A. J. What made it worse, he was Alfred Jacob Zander IV. There had *always* been an Alfred Jacob Zander around, and the family expected there always would be. Not if *he* had anything to say about it, there wouldn't. If ever he had a son, he wouldn't name him Alfred Jacob Zander V! Not in a million years, he wouldn't.

It would've been nice being a Rick or a Steve or even a Randy. Then he'd have used the whole name, instead of just initials. Maybe, he thought, when he was twenty-one he'd change his name to Tom or Jeff or something like that. Jeff Zander the *First*. It was something to think about.

Squinting, he peered through the windows. Eloise—Spence, rather—was staying in the far right lane and the cars and trucks and busses were passing the VW as though it were standing still. "We're just poking along," he complained, leaning forward. "What's the speedometer say, or doesn't *it* work, either?"

"It does," Spence answered. "Better'n forty-five."

"At this rate we'll never get there. Why don't you step on it?"

"I am," she said. "I've got it floored. Isn't that what you say, 'floored'?"

"Yeah, that's what you say." He flopped back in the seat again and let his head rest against the vibrating window and he thought about Eloise Ann Spencer. He didn't know quite what to make of her. Sure, she was good-looking, even

though he wished she'd let her hair grow. He liked girls with long hair, but hers was short and chopped off and shaggy, and he'd never seen her so much as run a comb through it. On her, though, it looked pretty good, he had to admit. In a way she resembled that lady flyer. Amelia Earhart? Yeah, that was her name. He laughed to himself. Amelia Earhart and Albert Schweitzer. Now, there's a weird couple for you. Spence's hair was the color of butterscotch topping—not quite red and not really blonde, either—and it seemed just the right color for her eyes, which were about as dark brown as any eyes he'd ever seen. They were so brown they were almost black.

It was good being with her and he had enjoyed their Saturday morning talks, even if she did have some peculiar ideas and kept talking about social awareness, and things like that. Of course he couldn't blame her for that because her father was at the university. Sociology. Or maybe it was psychology. Not that it mattered, because as far as he knew, those things were pretty much the same. Then A. J. thought about *his* father, Alfred Jacob Zander III. A. J. had always thought that his father did something sensible for a living. He was a stockbroker, and if a man was smart, there was plenty of money in that. Not like teaching. Eggheads. That's what A. J.'s father called college professors.

Sure, his father worried a lot and he grumbled plenty when the market was down, but he had had the guts to ride out the rough spells and it had paid off. Their cars were new, even if A. J. didn't get to drive them as much as he'd like, and the Zander home was like a picture in one of those beautiful house magazines his mother was always buying, and they lived as comfortably as anyone he knew. No, A. J. had no complaints.

Except right now. Right now he had plenty of complaints, far too numerous to mention. He loosed a deep sigh and,

wriggling his shoulders, he tried to get comfortable. He couldn't. He thought about his father and mother; sure, they were well fixed, they had enough money to live the good life now, but it hadn't always been that way. Both of them had been born toward the end of the Depression, and to hear them talk, it had been really tough.

Their families had had to scrimp and save and his dad never let A. J. forget that. His dad was always talking about knowing the value of money and being practical. "Take care of the pennies," he always told A. J., "and the dollars will take care of themselves." A. J. must've heard that a thousand times. Talk about corny. "You must learn to be more practical," his mother kept telling him. No matter what he did, he wasn't practical enough. Sometimes A. J. wished his family was poor, instead of being "comfortable," as his mother said. Or did he? He didn't really know. At least he wished they weren't so practical. It wasn't easy for him to be practical, the way his folks were. But that was just their way and there was nothing he could do about it. And he loved them, practical as they were.

Far ahead he could see the lights of Marana. Big deal. He closed his eyes and decided he wouldn't even think about how important it was to be practical, and even before they passed the Marana exit, Alfred Jacob Zander IV was sound asleep.

6

A. J. couldn't have been sleeping more than a few minutes, or so it seemed, when he awakened with a start as Spence pulled off the highway onto the shoulder and braked the VW suddenly. He stretched, yawned.

"What's the matter?" he asked, his voice thick with sleep.

"It's Gwendolyn," Eloise answered. "She was scratching on the window. That means she has to widdle."

"You mean she has to go to the bathroom?" asked the boy.

"People use bathrooms. Dogs widdle."

A. J. let the baby talk pass. He was too sleepy to get into

an argument about that. "But you can't pull over here on the Interstate just for a dog! It's for emergency parking only."

"When Gwendolyn has to widdle, that's an emergency. Especially if she's in the car."

"Then why didn't she go back at the gas station?" he asked.

"Probably because nobody asked her," Spence said as she jumped out of the car. She hurried around the VW and helped Gwendolyn jump off Mr. Tubbs's lap, then led her along the right-of-way. A. J. decided he might as well stretch his legs, too, and get away from that stinking saddle for a few minutes.

"What're we stopped for?" Mr. Tubbs called to A. J.

"So the dog can take a leak on the ground instead of on your lap," the boy answered.

"That's a right thoughtful dog," said the old man, and then he left the car, too.

"Why are *you* getting out?" A. J. asked.

"Figured I'd pee, too."

"You mean widdle," said A. J. "But didn't you just go at the gas station?"

"Shoot, that must've been the better part of an hour ago."

So the old man turned away from the road and undid his pants, just as if there were no cars passing by. A. J. turned and walked away so he wouldn't have to listen to the splashing.

The desert night was chilly and the boy was glad he had thought to bring his jacket, especially since they were heading up into the high country around Flagstaff. He looked up to the sky, but it was nothing but a mess of stars, so he closed one eye and looked through the single contact lens at the passing traffic. He wondered how long it would take them to get to Flagstaff and back doing forty-five miles an

hour. Too long, that was for sure. Forever, maybe. Saturday would be shot by the time they got back home. His parents would be furious; they always were when something upset the routine at home.

So lost in his thoughts was A. J. that he didn't even see the highway patrol car that had pulled up behind the parked Volkswagen until the red and yellow lights suddenly began flashing. This was it. So far they'd been lucky, but in time luck always runs out. The hairs rose on the back of his neck. They'll haul us back to town and to the police station—juvenile, if we're lucky—and they'll take our pictures and fingerprint us and then they'll lock us up and call our families. Really, he could get along without all that. It had to come though, he knew, because there was no other way this stupid thing could end. A. J. moved back a few steps, deeper into the shadows. Maybe the cop wouldn't see him at all.

Mr. Tubbs was still at it when the patrolman, in his Smokey the Bear hat, reached the car.

"Good evening," A. J. heard the patrolman say to Mr. Tubbs. The old man turned to see who was talking to him.

"Howdy, sonny," he said to the officer.

"Not supposed to park along the Interstate except in emergency, sir," the patrolman said.

"You'll have to talk louder," Mr. Tubbs said, touching an ear. "I'm some deef."

The officer cleared his throat and repeated what he had said.

"That so?" said Mr. Tubbs. "Ain't heard that."

"May I see your driver's license, please?"

"My what?"

"Driver's license."

"Reckon so," said the old man. "I ain't one to run afoul of the law. You'll have to help me, though." He asked the

policeman to climb into the rear of the Volks and fetch him the bedroll from behind the seat. The officer didn't duck low enough and knocked his hat to the ground.

As the patrolman brushed the dust from his hat, Mr. Tubbs dropped the bedroll onto the ground, hunkered beside it, and poked a hand inside. The officer shined his flashlight beam on the bedroll and presently Mr. Tubbs drew a worn leather wallet from inside the roll and from the wallet, produced a card. He handed it to the highway patrolman, who focused his flashlight on it.

"Well, I'll be . . ." said the officer, under his breath. And then, loudly, to the old man:

"Did you know your license had expired?"

"Yup."

"Expired in *nineteen twenty-seven?*"

"I reckon."

"Well, you should know better than to drive with an expired license!"

"Do know better, sonny," said Mr. Tubbs. "Ain't drove an auto*mo*bile since the twelfth day of November in nineteen and twenty-six—the very day I plowed plumb into a cow on the road. Gave me the fright of my life, cracked three ribs, and left a bump on m'head the size of an egg, plain ruint the boss's flivver, and killed the blasted cow outright! Right then I figured I'd do all my driving in a saddle, thereafter."

The officer's eyes narrowed. "Then if you aren't driving, who is?"

"The little missy—the one with the damn fool dog, over yonder."

Stepping back even farther into the shadows, A. J. fought hard to keep from laughing aloud.

"Hi," said Eloise Spencer, as she approached. "Is something wrong?"

The policeman turned and eyed her. "'Fraid there is, Miss," he said finally. "Parking is prohibited along the Interstate except in emergency."

"But it was an emergency," she said. "Gwendolyn here had to—well, relieve herself—and I was afraid that if she started going in the car I'd get all flustered and lose control of the auto and have an accident."

Gwendolyn wagged her tail and sniffed at the officer's leg. The highway patrolman raised his eyebrows and let out a deep breath. "I've heard a lot of excuses before, but that?" He shook his head. "How old are you, Miss?"

"Seventeen." She said it like she expected him to pin a medal on her, A. J. thought.

"May I see your driver's license?"

She got it from her wallet in the car and handed it to him. "Whose car is this?" he asked as he studied the license.

"My father's."

He nodded. "License looks in order," the officer said thoughtfully. Then, returning it to her, he added, "Just be careful, Eloise, and the next time the dog and the old man have to—you know—try to pull off in a rest area."

The girl promised she would.

A. J. realized there was no problem, so he stepped out of the shadows. He was grinning. The officer turned and shined his light in the boy's eyes. "You riding with them?" he asked. Then he glanced around. "Are there any *more* of you?"

"Yeah," A. J. said. Eloise frowned at him. "I mean, yes, sir. And no, sir. Yes, I'm with them, and no, there's no one else with us. Just three people and one dog."

"And she's doing the driving?" the patrolman asked, pointing at Eloise with his flashlight.

"She has to," A. J. said, pointing a finger at his eye. "I lost a contact."

Satisfied then, the patrolman nodded and raised his

flashlight, as if in a parting salute. "Okay," he told them, "have a good evening and keep the speed down." Touching his fingertips to the brim of his hat, he turned and headed for the patrol car.

"I'll remember, officer," Spence called after him, "and you have a good evening, too."

They climbed back into the VW and the patrolman waited until they had pulled away from the roadside before flicking off the flashing lights. He drove onto the highway behind them and followed their car more than a mile before pulling into the fast lane and passing them.

A. J. leaned forward. "Now drive carefully, young lady," he said sarcastically, "and remember what the cop said—keep the speed down." He laughed. "If that guy had really known how things were, he'd have told you to keep the speed *up*. Forty-five's the minimum speed on the Interstate—keep it floored or you'll get a ticket for poking along."

Spence didn't answer, so A. J. leaned back, crossed his arms over his chest, and tried to pick up that nap where it had been interrupted.

"You sleeping, A. J.?" she asked after a time.

He moaned. "Yeah, can't you tell?"

"I'm sorry, I didn't mean to wake you. I just felt like talking."

"So talk. I wasn't really sleeping, anyway. Just trying."

"Never mind."

"What do you mean, 'never mind'? You woke me up—or almost, at least—now you'd better tell me what's on your mind or I'll never forgive you." He leaned forward again, between the front seats, so that his chin almost rested on her shoulder. Mr. Tubbs and Gwendolyn were snoring.

"I was just wondering about you, A. J. You know, what you're interested in, what you like to do, things like that. I keep getting the feeling I hardly know you at all."

"For that you woke me up?"

"You weren't really sleeping, remember?"

"Yeah," he said. "Okay. I'm interested in eating—my mom's a great cook when she isn't experimenting with dishes that are supposed to be real healthy for you—and I'm interested in basketball."

"Are you on the team?"

"Past tense. You really know how to hurt a guy, don't you? I *was* on the team and all last year I played exactly four minutes, and that was in a game where we were leading eighty-seven to thirty-two and the coach emptied the bench. I quit at the end of the season and now I mostly mess around with the guys, playing pick-up games in the school yard near where I live."

"Eating and basketball? That's all?"

"What is this, anyway, some kind of a quiz show? What do I win if I give the right answer?"

"I'm just curious, A. J."

"Okay," he said, leaning back in the seat. "I like movies, too. Old ones, especially—the kind you see on the TV late show. You know, the old cop pictures and World War II movies and even the hokey old Westerns, with Randolph Scott and Gabby Hayes."

"It all sounds very uplifting," Eloise said.

"Don't blame me—you asked."

"I'm sorry, I didn't mean to cut you," she said. "How about later—what do you want to do?"

"You mean, what do I want to be when I grow up? Like a fireman or an astronaut or something?"

"All right, put it that way—what? But seriously?"

"I wish I knew. I don't have any idea, Spence. My dad wants me to go to the university and major in business administration and be a stockbroker, like he is. He thinks that's the greatest thing in life—being a stockbroker. But I

couldn't take it, sitting at a desk all day. So I don't know what I want to go in to, except that it won't be stocks and bonds, or whatever you call it."

"That leaves you a wide open field, doesn't it?"

"I guess." A. J. laughed. "Maybe I should be a cowboy when I grow up, like Mr. Tubbs here, only as played by Gary Cooper. Or Charlton Heston, maybe. Did you see him in *Will Penny?* That's got to be my all-time favorite Western. I must've seen it six times."

"Somehow you just don't seem the Charlton Heston-cowboy type," Spence said.

"Yeah, I guess you're right. I'm probably more like a Woody Allen trying to find himself. Woody Allen—you'd never catch him in a Western."

She didn't answer, and that suited A. J. just fine. He wriggled, trying to get comfortable next to that saddle, and finally gave up. His mind drifted, and he imagined himself—as played by Woody Allen—as a sidekick to Mr. Tubbs—as played by an old and toothless John Wayne—riding off into some faraway sunset. Of course old Mr. Tubbs had his legs wrapped around his trusty old saddle. A. J. patted the pommel of the saddle beside him and sneezed.

"Bless you," said Spence. A. J. didn't even thank her.

7

"My orange juice," said Mr. Tubbs.

"Beg pardon?" asked Eloise Ann Spencer, her eyes on the road.

"My *orange* juice," the old man repeated. "Ever' night before I go to bed the girl brings me a glass of orange juice. Didn't get any tonight."

"You want to go back and get it?" A. J. asked.

"Nope, don't reckon so. 'Sides, past time for orange juice back there."

It didn't make sense, A. J. thought, the old man getting cranky and fussing just because he'd missed having a lousy

glass of orange juice. Probably this was just another thing that happened to you when you got old. Crankiness. The boy shivered at the thought of it. At the thought of being old, like Mr. Tubbs, and fussing because you didn't get your bedtime orange juice. He couldn't remember Mrs. Koplin's being cranky like that, but maybe she had been. It was so long ago that there wasn't a whole lot about her that he did remember.

"Being old must be awful," he said then, loud enough so Mr. Tubbs could hear.

"Don't mind it particularly," the old cowboy said, giving his shoulders a shrug. "A man don't hardly have no choice in the matter. It just happens. 'Sides, it is a damn sight better'n *not* gettin' old." Mr. Tubbs chuckled at what he had said and the laugh became a cough. The dog stirred on his lap.

After a few moments the boy spoke again. "I don't know," he said. "I mean, when you're old—you know, *really* old—what's there to look forward to? I mean, I like having things to look forward to, like Christmas and going on vacation in the summertime and school dances. Things like that. But when you're old and you don't have *anything* to look forward to—well, it must be awful sad."

"Just what do you mean, *nothin'* to look forward to, sonny?" asked Mr. Tubbs, turning his head so he could see A. J. "Got plenty to look forward to. Why, ever' night I go to bed and look forward to wakin' up the next mornin', and when I do, I'm pleased as pie with myself."

The boy wasn't really listening to what Mr. Tubbs was saying. He was thinking. "The Apaches," A. J. said in time, "now *they* had the right idea. In social studies Mr. Phelps was telling us about how when an Apache got old, too old to keep up with the rest of the band, he'd just announce to everybody one morning that he was taking off.

"And he'd pack up some water and food—jerky, I guess—and wander away into the desert someplace to die. And if the old guy didn't have the guts to do it himself, the others would give him some food and tell him to get lost, because he was slowing them down, and so the old guy would take the hint and drop out of sight and go off somewhere by himself and die."

Mr. Tubbs turned his head away from the boy and faced forward again. He cleared his throat, as if he was going to say something, but he didn't. The old man sat quietly, staring straight ahead through the windshield.

"And the Eskimos—I hear they set their old people afloat on hunks of ice, or something, and they say even elephants know enough to go off to a place where there's quicksand, and they just step into it and disappear, so that the young elephants don't have to worry and take care of them."

"Dr. Hickman told me that it looks as though I'll be getting my braces off by Christmas," Spence said, cutting off A. J. before he could continue. She was almost shouting. What the heck did her braces have to do with Apaches or elephants or with orange juice, for that matter? the boy wondered. Sometimes he just couldn't figure girls out.

Crap. If they didn't want to hear his stories he wouldn't waste his energy telling them. He scrunched down in his seat, pouting. There was less traffic now. It must be getting late. At least it seemed late. He yawned and wished he was in his comfortable bed at home, instead of in the back seat of an old VW. It was a heap, and he didn't like those dinky foreign cars, anyway. His father often talked about how unsafe they were. He'd take a big, American-built car, any day. This one was really ancient. Why, chances were Hitler was still in power when it rolled off the assembly line in Germany. The thought tickled A. J. and he chuckled to

himself. He started to lean forward to tell Spence, but then he thought she'd start talking about her braces and wouldn't get the joke, so he settled back in the seat again. The saddle's pommel poked him just below the ribs and he swore softly to himself.

That car. The white paint of the exterior was dull and looked as though it hadn't been washed, let alone polished, for years, and there were so many tiny dents and creases that the fenders almost looked quilted. The upholstery must have been in horrible shape, because the seats were covered with washed-out striped serapes from some cheap curio shop down on the Mexican border. It surprised A. J. that the car had made it as far as the city limits of Tucson, and he was convinced there was no way it would get them to Flagstaff, let alone back home again. A clunker. There was no other way to describe it, unless you called it a *beat-up* old clunker. Only thing in miles around older than the car is Mr. Tubbs, he thought, and again he chuckled to himself.

"There's your orange juice up ahead," Spence told Mr. Tubbs.

"Where?" the old man asked, leaning forward to gaze through the windshield. "Don't see no orange juice."

"I mean there's an exit coming up and the sign said 'Food' and 'Services.' That means a restaurant. We'll stop and get you some orange juice."

"Oh, for—you mean to say we're going to stop again? We'll never get there," A. J. protested. "I had figured this was going to be a quick round trip, like you said, but it's turning out to be a career. If we aren't stopping to widdle, we're stopping to fill up on orange juice so we can stop to widdle again! Cripes!"

A lot of good his protest did. They took the exit ramp to

the access road, then followed it a half mile or so, past a service station and some businesses that were closed up for the night. Spence pulled up and parked in front of a place that was part tavern, part cafe, and turned off the engine.

"Looks fine to me," she said brightly. "Bet they pour a good glass of orange juice here."

"Looks like a dump to me," disagreed A. J. He was suspicious of roadside cafes that were not national chain restaurants. "We'll probably all get ptomaine."

"Don't want chow mein," piped in Mr. Tubbs. "Don't like it, never have. Me, I'm a meat and potatoes man."

"He didn't say *chow* mein," Eloise said, raising her voice. "What he said was *pto*maine. That's food poisoning."

"Never mind, them Chinee dishes is all the same. Once we had us a Chinaman cook out to the ranch and all the boys was about to up and quit because all he'd rustle up was them dishes with foo and gum and chow and sub and chop in their names. Finally learned how to burn a proper 'Merican beefsteak, so the boss kept him on. Learned how to make a proper apple pie, too, that old son of a gun. Yick Yee—yup, that was his name."

"Reach behind the seat and see if you can find Gwendolyn's water dish," Spence said to A. J. "That poor dog must be dying of thirst." The dog saw the dish and sat up on Mr. Tubbs's lap, her fat tail wagging and thumping against the old man's arm. "Be right back," the girl said, and she ran toward the restaurant, returning, in a short time, carefully carrying the green plastic bowl. She put it on the ground beside the car, opened the door, and grabbed the leash. The dog needed no coaxing to get her to jump to the ground.

As Gwendolyn drank noisily, Mr. Tubbs straightened his Stetson and brushed at the dog hairs on his Levi's. When

Gwendolyn had had her fill of water, Eloise put the dog back in the car, rolled the windows open a few inches, and locked her inside. They entered the cafe then.

The walls and ceiling were of yellow knotty pine and on the walls were oil paintings on black velvet of desert vistas and religious scenes, and mounted sets of steer horns, all for sale. A. J. made a mental note not to order a hamburger. You always had to worry about ground meat in roadside places like this, especially if they had steer horns for decoration. From the jukebox a country-western tune blared loudly, and the sound of loud talk and laughter came from beyond the swinging doors that led to the bar. He hated kicker music and tried to shut his ears to the sound of it.

They sat at a table with a floral-patterned plastic cover on it. "Evening," said the waitress, placing three plastic water tumblers on the table. "You all want to see menus or do you know what you'd like?"

"We'll take menus," A. J. said, brushing at a scatter of spilled sugar in front of him. Turning his head, A. J. watched the waitress as she went for the menus.

She was probably fifty, at least, wore too much make-up, and her hair was dyed an awful, bright red. "Brassy," was the word his mother used to describe a woman like her. She brought the menus, dropping them on the table, and walked off. A hard one, thought A. J.

He closed the eye without the contact lens and squinted at the menu. Nothing sounded good. "I think I'm just going to have something to drink," he said.

"Me, I'd like the steak and eggs with hash browns," said Mr. Tubbs. "Can't, though."

"Sure you can, Mr. Tubbs," said Eloise. "Anything on the menu—if you really want it, go ahead and order it."

"Can't," said the old man. He opened his mouth wide and pointed his finger into it. A. J. saw a tongue and plenty

of gums, and that's all. "Forgot my teeth back to the home. They was in the glass on the table 'side my bed."

"You mean to say you remembered that dumb saddle and forgot something important like your teeth?" A. J. sneezed. The saddle. He shouldn't have mentioned it.

Mr. Tubbs glowered at him from beneath his bristly eyebrows. Before he could answer the boy, the waitress returned and stood with pen raised over her pad.

"We're not any of us hungry," Spence said, "so I guess we'll just have something to drink."

"You want a cola?" A. J. asked her.

"I told you," she said, "my dermatologist told me cola's bad for acne. I'll have iced tea."

"Well, bring *me* a cola," said the boy, "and Mr. Tubbs here—he wants orange juice. Small."

"Damned if I do," said Mr. Tubbs. "Bring me coffee, ma'am."

"I thought the only reason we stopped here was because you said you wanted orange juice," A. J. said.

"Didn't say that. Said that every night the girl *brings* me orange juice. Can't tolerate the stuff. Minute she's out of my room I pour it down the toilet."

"*Mis*-ter Tubbs," said Eloise, teasingly. The old man cackled.

"Must be the healthiest toilet in Arizona, getting all that Florida sunshine," A. J. said.

The waitress brought their drinks and Mr. Tubbs opened five little envelopes of sugar—A. J. counted them—and emptied them into his coffee. Then he poured cream into the cup until it brimmed. Carefully he stirred the brew, and leaving the spoon in the cup, he raised it and sipped noisily.

"You never got married?" the boy asked Mr. Tubbs. No wife would ever have let him drink coffee *that* way. And all

that sugar—it was supposed to be bad for you. "You never had any kids?"

"Nope," said the old man. "No time. The years went by so quick I just never got around to it. Time came I began to think family, why, it was plumb too late. The hankerin' was long gone." He slurped a drink of coffee, then smiled.

"Oh, I had me some lady friends, make no mistake about that, but nothin' permanent, mind you."

"Now that you're—well, old and alone—don't you miss having had a family?" Spence asked.

He shook his head. "You don't rightly miss somethin' you never had. Man who never sank his teeth into a chunk of beefsteak in his life can't yearn for it, 'cause a mouth don't water for somethin' it ain't never tasted. 'Sides, don't reckon no woman would've put up with the likes of me." He drank again from the cup.

"Ain't got no regrets, way I figure it."

They were almost finished with their drinks when the waitress returned to the table with the check. She dropped it in front of A. J. and he pushed it over to Spence. Leaning over, the waitress nudged the girl's arm with her elbow.

"Which one's your date, honey," she asked in a voice loud enough for everybody to hear. "That skinny beanpole kid, or the cutie-pie in the Stetson?" A. J. saw her wink broadly at the girl, and Eloise laughed.

"C'mon," the boy said, "let's get going."

"Whoa, there, sonny, not so fast. I'd admire to have another cup of this fine coffee, if this here young lady'll be so kind." Mr. Tubbs looked up at the waitress and gave her a toothless smile. She brought the coffee pot and refilled the cup. As she turned from the table, Mr. Tubbs reached out and slapped her on the behind. She looked back and smiled at him over her shoulder, then returned to the counter.

"Son of a gun," said Mr. Tubbs as he began opening envelopes.

A. J. felt his face redden. He had never seen his father—or any other man, for that matter—slap a waitress on the bottom like that. Spence was blushing, too, he could see.

The boy pushed away from the table. "I'm going to use the men's room," he announced, "and then I'll wait for you outside." He paused for a moment, then spoke to the girl. "I wouldn't leave a tip, if I were you. She's just too wise."

Outside he leaned against the car. The night air was cool and fresh and it felt good. A. J. thought about what had happened at the table. Spence kept talking about what a "sweet old man" Mr. Tubbs was, but sweet old men didn't act that way. Nasty old men did. Or maybe that was the way cowboys always acted. Maybe they just went around slapping waitresses on the ass just to have something to do when they weren't branding calves or roping steers. He'd have to talk to Mr. Tubbs about keeping his hands to himself the rest of the trip.

In time the others came out of the restaurant. There was a lightness in Mr. Tubbs's step that A. J. hadn't noticed before, and he was still grinning that silly, toothless grin of his.

Old men, A. J. thought, and he shook his head. Nasty old men . . .

8

A. J. was glad that Spence had sense enough to walk Gwendolyn off into the desert beyond the parking lot before they started rolling again. Maybe that might save *one* stop along the way. Mr. Tubbs was in his seat and A. J. was all settled in the rear by the time the girl and dog returned to the VW. That saddle smelled worse every time he got back into the car. Whether it smelled of horse or man or both, he couldn't be sure. One or the other alone just couldn't smell *that* bad by itself. He sneezed. All he had to do was think of that saddle and he sneezed.

Once they were moving the boy looked out the window,

but there wasn't much to see except for an occasional distant light or a passing auto. Thrilling. Even in the daylight there wasn't a lot to look at from the highways of southern Arizona. Just mountains and desert, and if you've seen one saguaro cactus, you've seen them all. He was bored.

"Why don't you turn on the radio?" he suggested.

"Can't," answered the girl. "It hasn't worked since I was in the fourth grade."

"Lovely," said A. J.

"There are three of us," she said. "Maybe we could sing 'Row, Row, Row Your Boat,' in parts."

"Skip it," the boy told her. "I'll sleep."

"Well, maybe Mr. Tubbs can tell us one of his stories," Spence countered. "I never did hear how you came to be a cowboy and what it was like in the old days and all." She placed her hand on the old man's arm and patted it.

"Shoot," he said, "ain't a whole lot to tell." Taking off his Stetson, he gave his head a good scratch. "Wouldn't hardly know where to begin."

For almost a mile they drove in silence as the old man collected his thoughts. Or maybe he was dozing, A. J. supposed. Old people were always dozing. But then Mr. Tubbs chuckled.

"We was always funnin', us boys was, ever' chance we had. 'Member one time we was in Flagstaff of a Saturday afternoon and we was in the most elegant eatin' and drinkin' place in town, washin' down the trail dust with a few beers.

"Well, that ol' place served up fancy meals and it happened a couple of dudes come in. Bunch of us was standin' at the bar doin' our damnedest to drink Flagstaff dry and them dudes, they took one of the tables not far from us. We figured 'em for drummers—travelin' salesmen fellers— their clothes bein' all spiffy and citified and their hair

slicked down with that sweet-smellin' stickum.'' The old man paused, as if he had forgotten his story.

"And then what happened, Mr. Tubbs?" Eloise asked.

"Plenty," chuckled the old man. "Now, us boys stood there mindin' nobody's business but our own, but we couldn't help noticin' them dudes and hearin' all their complainin'. Seems nothin' suited 'em.

"The whiskey was rotgut, they said, and it weren't fit for drinkin', an' the beer—well, the beer wasn't cold enough. They decided then they was goin' to eat some beefsteaks and fried potatoes for dinner, that bein' the speciality of the house. Well, the barkeep—he done the table-waitin' hisself—brought 'em their food and they commenced to complain worse'n before. Steak was tough and the potatoes was raw and greasy and the biscuits, they was stale. Not fit to feed to dogs back home in New York City, they complained. So then they started bad-mouthin' the Territory of Arizona and Flagstaff and the West an' 'bout ever'thing and ever'body they could think of.

"Me'n Dutch, we'd heard enough of their ornery talk, so he winked at me and gave me the elbow and I followed him out of the place.

"Couple doors away was a butcher shop, and a sign in the front window said they was sellin' fresh beef that day. We went inside and talked to the butcher feller and told him what we was up to and the butcher, he just roared laughin' and took us out back to where he done his butcherin'. Said he'd slaughtered a cow that very mornin' and invited us to help ourselves.

"So me'n Dutch, we dipped our arms into that big ol' washtub back there that had fresh cow's blood in it, and we rubbed it on our arms and splashed some on our clothes, us laughin' the whole while. Then we went back to that elegant

place where them dudes was eatin'." Chuckling, Mr. Tubbs shook his head.

"Well, when we walked into that saloon all bloodied up as we was, 'course the whole place quieted down. Us two walked slow as you please, lookin' our meanest, up to the bar, not more'n a dozen feet from where them dudes was sittin'. I dropped a twenty-five-cent piece onto the bar and then, in a gruff voice loud enough so's nobody could help hearin' it, ol' Dutch, he says, 'Barkeep,' he says, 'jist make it a couple beers. Weren't hardly worth the effort—that ol' son-of-a-gun dude didn't have but two bits in his pockets.'

"Shoot, you never in your life saw nobody move faster'n them two New York City fellas did. Why, they dropped a couple dollars on the table and made for the door, 'bout stumblin' one over the other, and was through them batwing doors quicker'n a man could say, 'good riddance.' Shoot," the old man said, "that Dutch, he was a dandy, a genuine heller. We sure had us some good times together. Anymore, things ain't the way they was in them days." Then he was silent again.

They all laughed and then Eloise asked Mr. Tubbs how old he was when he came West.

"Younger'n that sprout in the back seat," Mr. Tubbs answered, "and a mite smarter, too, if I say so myself.

"Born and raised up on a farm in Champaign County in Illinois, I was. Richest farmin' soil anyplace in the world, I expect. Wasn't many years before I come to find out that rich or no, workin' the soil weren't for me. I weren't cut out to be a dirt farmer.

"I was plenty restless an' I had managed to put aside a few dollars and one evenin' I told my ma I was leavin'. 'Course she bawled, me bein' the baby of the family, but she seemed to understand, and shoot, there was seven brothers all older'n me, and every last one a better farmer'n

ever I'd hope to be. Pa—him I could never face to shake his hand and tell him I was off, though. He just wouldn't 've understood. So that night I bundled my few belongin's and set out." The old man fell silent. "You know," he said finally, "I'd been readin' them dime novels about all the excitement and adventures them cowboys was havin' out West, and I reckoned I'd see for myself."

"Well, was it?" A. J. asked. "Exciting, I mean?"

"Shoot, no. Why, after I'd been on the road for a month or two and found myself in Flagstaff, here in Arizona Territory, doin' odd jobs to keep my belly from growlin', someone pointed out Mr. Pfeffer to me and said he was one of the biggest ranchers in this country and that he was mean as a stepped-on sidewinder. Well, I pulled myself up tall as I could and hauled back my shoulders and marched right up to him like he was anybody else, and I asked was he hirin'? and son of a gun, he laughed and signed me on right there and then, sayin' I appeared a mite young, but that he admired a feller with spunk. So that, I reckon, is how I happened to become a cowboy. I rode with old Mr. Pfeffer and then his son and then *his* son, and in time he up an' sold the place and put me out to pasture in that there rest home."

"But what about all that adventure and excitement?" A. J. wanted to know.

"Weren't none. Only work, hard work. Started in at thirty-a-month an' keep and worked my way up to fifty-five-a-month." He paused, then continued. "Time came, though, when I couldn't do a whole lot of ridin', but they kept me on anyways. I puttered about the house doin' mostly woman chores, and presently there wasn't much else I could do but set an' mend harness.

"Shoot, that Pfeffer place must've had the mendedest harnesses in all of Arizona, but you know, funny thing is, we hadn't used a whole lot of harnesses for a good many

years. Trucks an' them Jeep cars was what they got to usin' mostly, 'stead of horses, but I kept sittin' there, mendin' them ol' horse harnesses over and over, earnin' my keep."

"How can you afford to live in that rest home?" asked A. J. "It costs a bundle—I know, I heard my folks talking about it."

"The second Mr. Pfeffer I worked for—he done it. He wrote it right there in his last will and testament that I should be took care of in a nice place, come the time I needed it. When he up an' died an' his son took over and then sold out, why, they put me in that there rest home.

"Shoot, though, I weren't ready to rest. I knowed full well a time was comin' when I'd be headin' for the *long* rest, an' me, I wanted to keep kickin' up my heels long as I could."

"Don't you like it where you are?" Spence asked.

"Nope, not one bit," he said. "Food's awful—'bout ever'-thing tastes the same, like creamed wheat, and there ain't a bottle of hot-pepper sauce in the whole blasted place, an' if a man has a mind to spend a Saturday night in a saloon, he's plumb out of luck.

"An' all them ol' people they got livin' there—they're different. Drive a man loco, they will. City people," Mr. Tubbs said, as if that explained everything. "Ain't one of 'em knows what it's like to have lived a life ridin' them mountain meadows and seein' the sun come up ever' mornin' and seein' it set of an evenin', come summer or winter. Nope, they ain't my kind of folks.

"An' them fool nurse ladies—they keep callin' me, '*we*'! 'Did *we* sleep good?' an', 'Did *we* have our bath yet, Mr. Tubbs?' an' 'Have *we* had our bowel movement yet today?' Busybody women—ain't no concern of theirs whether *we* had us a crap—sorry, missy—or not!" Eloise and A. J. laughed.

"What about your family?" the girl asked. "Did you ever go back to Illinois to visit them?"

Mr. Tubbs shook his head. "Nope," he said, "never did. Oh, I kept in touch, all right. I wrote home. Wrote home once a year whether I had any news to tell or not. An' Ma, she wrote back once a year, too, faithful as a ma could be. An' then I started bein' awful busy—seems there was always somethin' for me to be doin'—an' them letters didn't get wrote regular as they should and presently, well, I just plain lost touch."

"When was that?" Eloise asked. "That you lost touch, I mean?"

Rubbing his whiskery chin with his big fingers, he thought for a moment. "Must've been right after the war—the big'un. I'd say maybe nineteen an' nineteen. Twenty, maybe. Ever since, I reckon my only family's been Mother Nature and Father Time, an' them two I come to know right good."

It was then that Mr. Tubbs decided he hadn't been to the bathroom for a while and he asked Spence to pull over. A few miles up the Interstate they came to a roadside rest area and she pulled off the highway. "Didn't you go back at the restaurant?" asked A. J. "That's only ten or fifteen miles back down the road."

The old man shook his head. "Nope," he said, "had no hankerin', then."

If it wasn't the dog, it was the old man, thought A. J. He wished they'd at least get on the same schedule.

The area was bright with overhead floodlights, and several trucks and cars were parked there, many of their occupants sleeping. There were some shelters with picnic tables under them and a cement block restroom with one side for women, the other for men. A. J. steered Mr. Tubbs to the restroom, then walked back to Spence, who had the dog on

a leash. Gwendolyn's nose was to the ground, sniffing, and they followed her.

"Bassets sure do sniff a lot," the boy said to Eloise.

"I know," she said. "Way back, they're part bloodhound. A. J.," she said then, a question in her voice, "can I ask you something?"

"Sure," he told her. "What is this, quiz time again?"

"I'm serious, A. J. It's about Mr. Tubbs. Don't you like him?"

Surprised, he looked at her. "What do you mean, don't I like him?"

"Oh, I don't know, it's just that you seem—well, sort of sharp with him. Impatient, maybe."

The boy toed a small pebble loose from the earth, then kicked it.

"He's okay, I guess, for an old guy. If I found out I had to be stranded on a desert island for the rest of my life and I could take one person with me, I'd never in a million years pick him." He grinned. "*You,* maybe, but not him."

"Thanks a lot," she said.

"Don't get the idea I hate him or even dislike him or anything like that," the boy said. "It's just that he's just not one of my very favorite people. You know, he's a pest, cranky, and having to be cooped up in that dinky car with him is getting to me."

"But he's a sweet old man, A. J., and he has so little time left."

"Maybe that's it right there—he's old and doesn't have much time left, and being around old people gives me the creeps."

"*All* old people? How about your grandparents?"

"There's only Gramps, and you know how he is. I really hate to have to go visit him there in the nursing home. That's why, when I met you and we started talking every

Saturday, it didn't seem too bad anymore. My other grandparents, though, I never knew.''

Squatting, he scratched Gwendolyn behind her ears. She wagged her tail, flopped down, and rolled over to have her belly rubbed. She purred, almost like a cat, and for nearly a minute the boy said nothing as he scratched the dog. "I don't know what it is, Spence," he said finally.

"It's just like I told you. I feel spooky when I'm with old people and I can't help it. They're so—oh, I don't know— useless. They've lived their lives and all they do is sit in rocking chairs and rock and talk about their grandchildren and great-grandchildren and about how wonderful it was in the old days when they were young and about how bad things are now, and they wait to die.''

"Mr. Tubbs—he doesn't sit and rock. He's not a rocking chair kind of person.''

"I know, you've said that before. So maybe he isn't, but he *is* old, God but he's old, and what's he doing that's useful, that's worthwhile?''

"He's led a very active, useful life.''

"That's it—*led*—past tense. Everything is past tense when you get old like him. There's no future tense, and not much of a present tense either, for that matter. It's all 'was' and 'did' but never 'will.' Everything is over for them, except dying.'' A. J. patted the dog's chest, then stood up, brushing his hands together.

"That's an awful way of looking at it," she said. "So it's not just Mr. Tubbs—it's *all* old people you don't like. Is that it, A. J.?''

"Maybe," he said, frowning and biting at his lip. "But it's not really that I don't like them. It's more that I feel sort of nervous when I'm around them, like maybe I can't trust them. I guess it was Mrs. Koplin . . .''

"Missus who?''

"Koplin." He paused and turned to the girl, eyeing her through the single contact lens. "I've never told anyone about it, because it's all so stupid, so weird. Spence, if I tell you, you won't tell anyone else, promise?"

"I guess," she agreed softly.

"Well, when I was little, real little, Mrs. Koplin used to live next door and she took care of me a lot, and even when she wasn't taking care of me, I'd go over to visit her. I hardly remember what she looked like, except that she was real old and sweet and I loved her because she was somebody special.

"When I'd hurt myself she'd take me in her arms and rock me and tell me that I'd be all right, and before long everything was better. She always had freshly baked cookies in her cupboard and every time I went to see her, I had two or three of them. And stories. Cookies and stories. I don't remember what any of the stories were about, but she always had a different one to tell, or maybe it was just one long story that went on and on as long as I knew her. They weren't the kind of stories you find in books, but they were about when she was small and living in the old country, wherever that was."

"She sounds wonderful, A. J.," Spence said as the boy paused. "I can't see why you don't like old people just because of her."

"Take it easy, I'm coming to that, but I have to sort it out in my mind and get it straight. It was all so long ago that it's kind of, you know, hazy. I'm not even sure what I actually remember and what my folks told me about her, later. And when I think about her I just see a little, bent old lady with gray hair, and except for her eyeglasses, I can't see her face at all, I can't put it into focus, but still I know that it's Mrs. Koplin."

Gwendolyn had stretched out in the dirt and was sleeping, and A. J. squatted down beside her again and patted

her. Though her eyes remained closed, her tail began to wag.

"I wonder what's keeping that old man?" he said. And then he looked up at Spence. "Are you sure you want to hear all this? It's so dumb."

She told him to go on.

"One time I went next door to see her and went inside— she always kept her back door unlocked—and she was taking a nap, so I climbed up on the bed and took a nap beside her, the way I did lots of times. It was almost like a game with us.

"After a while I woke up and she was still sleeping and I wanted a cookie and I wanted to hear a story, so I shook her and called her name, but she didn't wake up. I shook her again and she still didn't wake up. Her arm felt cold when I touched it, so I covered her with the blanket and got down from the bed and went home."

A. J. stood, jamming his hands into his pockets, and looked at Spence. "Well, I told my mother about Mrs. Koplin taking a long nap and she went next door and—well, Mrs. Koplin was dead. I watched from the front window of our house and the men from the undertaker's came and a while later they took Mrs. Koplin away.

"I asked Mom where Mrs. Koplin was and she just said that she had gone away, but I heard neighbors talking and they said that Mrs. Koplin was dead and when I asked my mother what dead meant, she said it just meant that Mrs. Koplin had gone away and that we wouldn't be seeing her anymore. I couldn't believe it, because I loved Mrs. Koplin and I knew that she loved me. But Mom was right, I didn't see her anymore. There were no more stories, no more homemade cookies, no more of her arms around me to make me feel better.

"It really hurt me, that Mrs. Koplin would do that to me. It was almost as though she had tricked me, going away like

that, and for a long time I couldn't understand, but then, when I was older, I learned what being dead meant. I understood then, but still I felt that Mrs. Koplin had—well, played that trick on me by leaving—and I got the idea in my head that old people did that to you, and so I guess I just haven't wanted to be around any of them . . ."

"But you can't feel that way, A. J.," Spence said. "You can't try to avoid getting involved with old people for fear they're going to die. It doesn't make sense."

A. J. opened his mouth to answer, but then saw the old cowboy coming toward them. "I guess while we're here I'll use the facilities," he said, and he walked past Mr. Tubbs on the path. Cripes, thought A. J., the old man walks out of the bathroom still trying to get his zipper pulled up, and with people all around. Old folks, he muttered. The boy stepped inside the restroom. The chemical toilet smelled terrible and he held his breath as long as he could.

When he was finished washing his hands he looked up into the mirror above the basin to comb his hair. With one eye closed he found the part and combed carefully. Then he ran his fingers gently through his hair so that it would look casual and rumpled. His hair was full and bushy, and in the pale light of the bare, overhead bulb, he paused to admire it.

The face he saw beneath the casually combed hair was a young face, and for a moment it pleased him, and then, leaning forward against the basin he brought his young face close to the mirror and he squinted at it through his single contact and tried to picture himself old. Old like Tubbs. Old, with a wrinkly, white face and no teeth. Old, with red, watery eyes. Old, with a head that was bald and with ears that stuck way out but could hardly hear. But it didn't work. No matter what he did, the face stayed young. The longer he stared at the face in the mirror, the more con-

vinced he was that it couldn't happen to him. He'd go on living forever and all that time he'd stay young, young like the *real* face in the mirror. He'd never get old; he wouldn't allow it. And he'd never die. Oh, maybe he'd let himself get old*er,* but never *old,* really *old,* like the cowboy. He, A. J., *would* find that Fountain of Youth that Ponce de Leon had spent all that time looking for. He laughed.

Glancing down at the comb still in his hand, he saw a stray hair caught in its fine teeth. Jerking it out, A. J. quickly dropped it into the basin, turned on the water full force, and watched the hair swirl down the drain. He couldn't be losing his hair. Not at his age. He was a kid. Sixteen. Besides, it was just one single hair. He laughed at himself. Imagination, that's all it was.

Then, looking up into the mirror again, he opened his other eye and the face he saw in the mirror went fuzzy, out of focus, like a blurry blob, and Alfred Jacob Zander IV shuddered, because *that* face in the mirror looked as though it *might* be old, and it worried him.

9

For some time they drove in silence with Gwendolyn and Mr.
Tubbs sleeping, Spence keeping her eyes on the road,
though yawning now and again, and A. J. scrunched in the
rear seat with the smelly saddle and his thoughts.

There was plenty on his mind. His folks, for one thing. By
now they must be awfully worried. He had never stayed out
all night like this. Always before he'd come home when he
was supposed to be home. They'd be frantic. Would they be
able to handle it? he wondered. Probably. They'd get a little
hysterical, of course, especially his mother, but they'd get
over it. His father was cool and practical, and he'd look at it

from the practical point of view, whatever that was. For a while he'd be grounded—that much he knew for sure—but in time everything would be smoothed over. He thought some more about his bed and how he wished he was in it where he belonged, all comfortable and sound asleep instead of spending the night curled up with a stinking saddle. That saddle! He sneezed. Why hadn't he had sense enough to bring his allergy pills?

His mind drifted then to college and he wondered what he should major in. Right then he couldn't get awfully interested in anything. But there was time to think about that later; he still had two more years of high school, so he didn't have to make up his mind tonight. So instead of college, he thought about Eloise. Spence. The longer he was with her the more he liked her. She was easy to be with. But at the same time he was beginning to feel something close to hate toward her for getting him into this mess. Anger maybe, not really hate. And he worried that the way he was acting toward Mr. Tubbs would antagonize her, and *that* he didn't want to happen. He would try to be nicer to the old man, starting right now. He would be a regular Albert Schweitzer. The boy wondered about Mr. Tubbs and what it was about him that he didn't like. Thinking about it, he knew that it wasn't *only* Mr. Tubbs who bothered him, but old people in general. Except for Gramps, of course. Gramps was different, Gramps was in a class by himself. Gramps he liked. Loved, of course.

A. J. thought hard about it and realized he had never really spent much time thinking about old people before Gramps was brought to Tucson and they had put him in that rest home to live, if you could call that living. Now that it was actually on his mind, he realized he'd never really *thought* about any old people before, and had never had much of anything to do with them, except for seeing them

on the street and at church and in supermarkets and places like that. But now with Gramps being the way he was and with having to visit him in the rest home where he kept seeing all those other pathetic old people, it had begun to bother him. Their lives were behind them and they were just *there,* just waiting to die. They were just so many Mrs. Koplins, and he didn't want anything to do with them. He didn't want to become involved personally with them, but he certainly was involved with that Mr. Tubbs! Mr. Tubbs—he was a bald old Mrs. Koplin, in washed-out Levi's! He didn't even want to think about the old cowboy.

So he thought instead about the car he hoped he'd soon get from his folks—unless this trip blew it for him—and he thought about how Spence would look without those braces and he thought about shooting baskets with the guys and he thought about a lot of other things.

One thing he didn't think about—at least he tried not to think about—was what had happened in the restroom back there when he had realized he was losing his hair. That, he tried to put completely out of his mind. After all, it was just *one* hair. Funny, the tricks your imagination can play on you.

Presently there were more lights off in the distance, and in time the Interstate widened by one more lane as they neared Phoenix. This was a little more interesting to look at than all that black nothing that they had been driving through. Traffic was heavier, too.

"Get in the middle lane and stay there," A. J. said, leaning forward.

"You're awake."

"How'd you guess?"

"Wise guy, I was just making an observation. You've been so quiet back there since the last stop that I figured you were either asleep or mad."

"Neither. I've been thinking."

"About what?"

"Lots of things."

"Like?"

"Like how expensive you must be. To your folks, I mean. You must cost them a bundle when the monthly bills come in, what with the dermatologist and the ornithologist and all."

"Ornithologist? I don't go to an ornithologist."

"Then who's straightening your teeth?" A. J. challenged.

"My *orthodontist*. An ornithologist studies birds."

"Yeah, I knew it was something like that. Anyway, you must cost a bundle."

"I think I'm worth it," she said laughing.

"That's a matter of opinion," he said, and he thunked a finger at the back of her head.

"Why do you go to a dermatologist, anyway? You don't even have any pimples."

"I don't have any because I'm awfully careful and I do exactly what my dermatologist tells me to do."

"Me, I don't have acne. Oh, I get a pimple once in a while, but only one at a time. Never more than one. Like now, I've got this one on my nose and before that I had one on my forehead, right here."

Eloise turned her head quickly to see where A. J.'s pimple had been.

"But now this one on my nose is going away," he continued, "and any day I guess I'll have one sprouting on my chin or my cheek or someplace else. I'll bet it'll be my cheek—it's overdue."

"Your system must be awfully well programmed."

"I guess so," the boy said. "What's he charge, about ten dollars for an office call? Your dermatologist?"

"Twelve."

The boy whistled. "And how often do you have to go?"

"Once a month unless I have a special problem, then I have to go oftener."

"So that's at least a hundred and forty-four bucks a year you pay the dermatologist. How about the orthodontist?"

"Honestly, A. J., I don't know these things! My folks never tell me and I never ask."

"You should ask. Aren't you interested in the important things? No—you must not be. You're not at all practical. Must be at least a couple of thousand, though. Dentists charge a bundle."

"Missy," put in Mr. Tubbs. "Can I ask you a personal question?"

A. J. saw Spence flinch, as if she were startled. "I guess so, Mr. Tubbs," she said hesitantly. "Just so it isn't *too* personal."

"About them teeth of yours—they're peculiar. Looks as though you got you a mouthful of barbed wire. Girl your age—it's a downright pity. Did you have some disease or somethin'?"

Eloise laughed. "Oh, no, Mr. Tubbs. A couple of my teeth came in sort of crooked and my dentist thought they should be straightened."

"So he went and put all that there hardware in your mouth?" The old man shook his head slowly. "Downright shame he had to go and do that. Spoils your looks. Reckon I'd as soon have crookedy teeth as go through life lookin' like that."

A. J. laughed. "She doesn't have to wear those braces *all* her life," he said. "Pretty soon they'll be taking them off and her teeth'll be just as straight as mine or yours or anybody's."

"Mine's mighty straight," said Mr. Tubbs, "whenever I think to wear 'em." He chuckled.

"Haven't your ever seen anybody with braces before?" asked Spence.

"Don't recall."

"How can anybody get to be a hundred years old and never have seen a person wearing braces?" A. J. said it more as a statement than a question.

"Easy," said Eloise. "He could live on a ranch out in the middle of nowhere, that's how."

"Besides, I ain't a hundred. Leastways, I don't think I am."

"Then how old are you?"

"Only the good Lord knows for sure," he said. "Me, I lost exact track long ago, but I reckon it must be ninety, ninety-five. Lord knows, maybe I *am* a hundred. When you get past the eighty mark, one more year don't matter a whole lot."

"Your birthday!" cried Spence. "We forgot all about it and it's a couple of minutes after midnight!" Keeping her left hand on the steering wheel, she reached sideways and pulled the old man toward her and planted a kiss on his cheek. "Happy birthday, Mr. Tubbs!"

"I thank you, missy. First time ever I been kissed by a lady with a mouthful of barbed wire."

"Seem any different?" asked A. J.

"Not so's I could notice." He paused, then spoke again. "'Course, it's been so long since I been kissed by *any* lady, barbed wire or no, that I've near forgot what it's like."

Spence broke into the happy-birthday song, then stopped abruptly. "Come on, A. J., I can't sing it alone."

"But I——" The girl didn't let him finish.

"A. J.," she said sharply, *"sing!"* A. J. sang. A lot of foolishness, he thought, but he sang anyway. When they were done, Spence started the song over and A. J. muttered "Cripes," and joined in. Talk about stupid—celebrating a

birthday when you're *that* old. Birthdays were for kids.

As they were finishing the second round the old man leaned suddenly forward, almost dumping Gwendolyn onto the floor of the car. The dog yelped and Mr. Tubbs hollered, "Hold on there!" Immediately the two stopped singing and Spence lifted her foot from the accelerator and touched the brake pedal.

"What is it?" the girl asked. "Is something wrong?"

"Nothin' wrong," said the old man, "'cept a friend o' mine—fella I used to ride with—he works up yonder at a place called the Bow-legged Cowpoke. Just saw a sign that said take the next exit."

"So you want to stop and see him?" asked Spence.

"Aw, come on now," A. J. protested. "It's after midnight. This is a heck of a time to make social calls."

Ignoring him, the old man said, "From what I heared a few years back, it's a saloon and eatin' place where they serve up cowboy beefsteaks and beans, an' them places stay open until all hours, I reckon. We had a postal card from him up to the ranch before we shut down, an' ol' Buck, he said to stop by any time and drink a beer with him."

"Buck?" asked A. J. "Your pal's name is Buck?" Half the cowboys that ever roped a cow must've been named Buck, he thought. Or Tex, or Slim.

"Ain't seen that boy in many a year," the old man said, looking over to Spence. "Shoot, I'd admire to stop by an' tell 'im howdy." There was a pleading tone in his voice.

"Then we'll just do that," said Eloise. "We'll stop by and see your friend. After all, it's your birthday!"

The old man chuckled with delight and slapped his knee, only he missed and hit Gwendolyn's rump, instead. She yelped again and A. J. groaned loudly, but said nothing.

Following the billboard signs along the roadways, Spence found the Bow-legged Cowpoke with no difficulty and

parked the car in the large, but nearly empty lot that surrounded the building. The restaurant had a Hollywood false front with a big sign over the front in that fancy frontier lettering.

With his parents, A. J. had eaten in a few similar places in Tucson. They were all the same. Red-and-white checkered plastic covers on all the tables, smelly kerosene lamps, waitresses in tight frontier pants, branding irons hanging on the walls, steak, beans, and salad on the menu. Climbing out of the car he could smell the aroma of mesquite smoke and cooked meat in the air and it made him think of food. His stomach growled.

As they walked toward the restaurant, a man stepped out of the main door and walked across the broad porch, down the few steps, and came slowly toward them. The boy squinted and could make out that the man was dressed in black western clothes, like a gunslinger in a cheap oat-burner, but he was older than any movie gunslinger he'd ever seen. Much older.

"Howdy, folks," he called as he neared them. "I'm the marshal of these parts. If you come to eat, I'm sorry— kitchen's done closed up for the night."

As the gunslinger approached, A. J. could see that he had a straggly, poorly kept beard that was patchy black and gray, and that he walked as though his feet hurt. Pinned to his black vest was a silver star, and holstered at his hip was a six-gun that looked suspiciously like a toy. Spurs on his boots jingled gently as he walked.

"We're not here to eat. We're looking for a man—Buck somebody," said Eloise.

The man in black stopped, frowned, looking from one to the other. His gaze settled on Mr. Tubbs. Fumbling in a shirt pocket, he pulled out a pair of plastic-framed eyeglasses, put them on, and leaned forward again.

"Why, you mangy, lop-eared, mule-headed, sawed-off,

near-sighted son-of-a-gun—how in the hell are you, Bucky boy?''

''Baldy Tubbs, by God!'' said the one in black, as though he didn't believe it. ''Why, I figured you was long ago dead an' buried, you ol' codger!''

They pumped each other's hands until A. J. thought their arms might fall off.

''Why you ornery sidewinder—I ain't felt better in years,'' Mr. Tubbs answered.

For what seemed to A. J. to be at least a minute, Buck looked at Mr. Tubbs, just shaking his head. There was a strange look in his eyes, as if he didn't believe he was actually seeing his old friend after all those years. Finally he cleared his throat and spoke.

''I'd ask you to step inside and drink a beer,'' he said, ''but the eatin' side's shut down an' the barkeep's fixin' to close up the saloon right quick.''

''Maybe 'nother time, Bucky boy,'' said Mr. Tubbs, ''but we're headed up north to the Pfeffer place, me'n my young friends here.'' He waved his hand toward Spence and A. J. ''She's missy and him—he's the kid. The kid's granddaddy,'' he added, ''is a good friend o' mine, down to the place where I'm bunkin'. Young'uns, say how-do to ol' Buck!'' The *kid,* thought A. J. That's me—Alfie the Kid, armed and considered dangerous. The least the old man could do is call me by my name.

''Howdy,'' said the marshal, tipping his black, broad-brimmed hat toward the girl. ''I'm proud to make your 'quaintance.''

''You own this here place?'' asked Mr. Tubbs.

Buck frowned and shifted uncomfortably. ''Well,'' he said finally, ''not rightly so, though you might say I sort of run the outfit. The boss, he calls me his ramrod and his public relations man.''

"That's a mighty high-falutin' soundin' job," Mr. Tubbs said.

"Mostly what I do is, I step out here an' meet the folks an' make 'em feel to home, and I let the tourists take my picture with each other, an' I josh with the li'l folks an' let 'em touch my badge and I show 'em my six-gun. An' when the place gets crowded, I tell the customers where to park their cars. How 'bout you, Baldy—you still workin'?"

"Shoot no," Mr. Tubbs said. "Young Pfeffer—he up an' sold the spread plumb out from under me, few years back, an' me, I got put out to pasture in an ol' folks home down to Tucson."

"Ain't you a lucky one, havin' three squares, a place to lay your head of a night, bein' able to warm your ol' bones in the sunshine, an' not havin' to put in a day's work . . ." The man in black shook his head.

"Mean to say you're workin' 'cause you *got* to?" asked Mr. Tubbs.

"That's 'xactly what I'm sayin'," Buck told the other. "Why, after I left the Pfeffer ranch I drifted on to New Mexico an' then Colorado an' Wyomin' and Lord knows where else. Never was able to lay aside a nickel for when I couldn't ride no more. Lucky I come across this here place. They keep me an' let me sleep on a cot out back in the shed and now an' again, the boss, he'll slip me a dollar or two.

"My feet is tired, I got the miseries in my back, an' I'm stove up from head to foot, an' there ain't nothin' for me to do but keep on workin'. Most likely I will till the day they plant me in a pine box."

A. J. noticed that the marshal's hands were trembling. He looped his thumbs over his fancy wide belt and that stopped the shaking.

"How about Social Security?" the boy asked. "Or welfare?"

Buck laughed. "Them little two-bit places I rode for didn't put no stock in that Social Security, and besides, I ain't rightly been on a proper payroll long enough, ever. An' as for welfare—well, I still got my pride. Figure as long as I can do a job of work, I'll keep doin' it."

"You hanker to head up north with us and have a look at the Pfeffer place?" asked Mr. Tubbs.

"Nope," Buck answered. "They might hire on somebody else here, and besides, I was only up there a couple years—not like you, Baldy. You stayed put. Me, I drifted."

"There was so many boys come and gone all them years, it's hard to remember sometimes," Mr. Tubbs said. Brightening then, he asked, "Was you up to the ranch when ol' Lonnie got tooken suddenly drunk first day of spring roundup and kep' fallin' off his horse?"

Shaking his head, Buck brushed his beard with trembling fingers. "Nope," he said. "That must of been 'fore my time. Why, you was already an ol' man, bald as a crick rock, an' me, I wasn't hardly dry behind my ears, time I signed on to ride for Pfeffer."

"Then you wasn't there, neither, time me'n Dutch put that salt in ol' Yick Yee's sugar, an' ever'thing he cooked turned out——"

"Nope, heard about that, though," said Buck, "an' heard how he took out after you boys with his meat cleaver an' chased you crost half of Coconino County, and wouldn't let you'n Dutch sit to table for a week."

Both old men laughed. "Them days was good'uns," Mr. Tubbs said wistfully. "They was indeed."

For a time the four stood silently. A. J. squinted and impatiently looked at his watch. The others ignored him.

"This here work you're doin' here—it ain't real cowboyin', then?" Mr. Tubbs asked.

"Ain't sat a horse for better'n fifteen years—'fraid to, I'm so stove up."

"An' that badge? You ain't a genuine lawman, neither?"

Buck laughed. "It's purely for the kids, for them tourists from back East who come out here wantin' to see the Wild West. They take a fancy to it. The badge, it's from the five-an'-ten-cent store, and this here gun," he said, patting the holster, "you look close enough an' you'll see it's a toy, too.

"Why, here I am, a growed-up man goin' on seventy-three years, an' I'm playin' with toys like a snotty-nosed calf." Buck's hands were trembling more than ever now and he stuffed them into his pockets. "But the tourists—they like to get their picture took with a real cowboy, an' the food's passable, an' I got me a place to sleep."

As he spoke, the floodlights on the top of the building suddenly went black, leaving the parking lot in darkness. A young man wearing a white apron stepped onto the porch and called out.

"C'mon, marshal, quit the gabbin' an' get your ass in here," he said. "You still got your moppin' to do, an' I want to close up an' get out of here."

Buck shut his eyes tightly and lowered his head.

"Do they make you do the mopping, too?" asked Spence.

"Yup, I'm the swamper, too. Got all likes of 'sponsibilities here, it seems. Well, I reckon I better get it done so's the barkeep can go home."

He pulled off his hat and ran his fingers through his stringy gray hair. "Pleased to meet you young'uns," he said to the boy and girl. His handshake was like a wriggling trout.

"Baldy, you ol' coot, you take care now, hear?" Again the two old men pumped hands. "An' next time you stop by, make it earlier so's I can buy you a beer."

"Wisht you could go up to the spread with us, Bucky boy."

"'Nother time," said the other.

"Well then, I'll be seein' you," said Mr. Tubbs, and the marshal nodded, put on his hat, and walked back toward the restaurant. He walked slowly, A. J. thought, as though it wasn't just tired feet bothering him. The spurs hardly jingled at all. The three stood watching the man in black as he mounted the steps, crossed the porch, and walked inside.

He didn't look back at them once, but Mr. Tubbs waved to Buck, anyway.

10

Now, as they drove through Phoenix, the traffic was heavier on the Interstate, even though it was well after midnight. Where was everybody going? Home, probably. Home from wherever they'd been. He sighed. That's just where he'd like to be going, too. Home. And the old man—that's where *he* should be, too, instead of out making social calls on old buddies in the middle of the night. The two of them—Mr. Tubbs and Buck—had been a lot younger when they had ridden together. A. J. wondered what Mr. Tubbs had been like when he was young. It was hard to picture him as a young man, a young cowboy. And Buck, the phony marshal

with the dime-store badge and the toy gun in his holster, it was almost harder to picture *him* being young and not having trembly hands. A. J. felt sorry for Buck, even sorrier for him than for Mr. Tubbs. Mr. Tubbs had an easy life now and everything was taken care of for him in the home, but poor old Buck, up in his seventies and really seeming sickly, still had to work to keep alive. But then Buck had drifted and had gone different places and seen things, done things, and now he lived in a shed behind a restaurant, with nothing but his memories and the few dollars his boss gave him. And Mr. Tubbs, who had worked all his life at one job, one place, was sitting pretty. The boy couldn't decide which would be worse. With one hand resting on the saddle's pommel, A. J. sat quietly, his fingers drumming on the saddle, thinking about how Buck must feel, being a pretend cowboy and entertaining the kids and telling people where to park their cars, when for most of his life he had been a *real* cowboy. He wanted to say something to Mr. Tubbs about his friend, but Mr. Tubbs hadn't spoken a word since they got back into the car, so A. J. said nothing.

Gwendolyn sat up just then, looked around the darkened auto, reached out a paw, and began scratching on the window with her nails. The noise bothered A. J., like fingernails on a blackboard.

"Shoot," said Mr. Tubbs, "she's got somethin' on her mind again an' I sure don't hanker for it to happen on *my* lap." He shifted uncomfortably. "Pull over, missy!"

"But, we can't pull over to the side of the Interstate going through Phoenix," the boy warned.

"Then what should we do?" asked Eloise.

"Do? Step on it, and don't get nervous."

"You know very well we're going as fast as we can."

"Then we'd better, all of us, start praying," the boy said. He laughed. "This is funny," he said.

"Wouldn't seem funny to you, sonny, if this here fat dog was sittin' on *your* lap," said the old man, "about to do what she's about to do."

Gwendolyn scratched more and there was urgency in it.

"I'm *hurrying,* I'm *hurrying,*" the driver said to the dog. Presently they left the heavy congestion of the city behind them and there was less traffic now and fewer lights. The scratching continued.

"I'm sorry," Eloise said finally. "We can't have Gwendolyn widdling on Mr. Tubbs, especially on his birthday. I'm going to pull over here and chance it." She eased the car over to the edge of the road, put it in neutral, pulled on the emergency brake, and ran around the car to Gwendolyn. The boy and the old man remained in the car.

"Hand me my bedroll, if you please, sonny," said the cowboy. A. J. hauled it out of the compartment behind him and handed it over the seat. Mr. Tubbs took something from it and poked it into his mouth.

"That something to eat you got there?" asked A. J. His stomach had been grumbling with hunger ever since the steak house, with its aroma of mesquite-broiled steak.

"Some might eat it," he said, "though it ain't hardly advisable."

"Then why'd you stick it in your mouth?"

"To chew, sonny. It's tobacco. Try some?" He handed the package to A. J., who closed one eye and studied it in the glare of passing headlights. Beechnut. He'd seen it in the drugstore plenty of times, but he'd never seen anyone buy any or *chew* any. He sniffed it.

"What's it like?"

"Some milder'n the plug I chewed when I was a lad your age, but not much milder. You take a pinch of this in your mouth and you know you got you some tobacco there."

A. J. wrinkled his nose and passed the Beechnut back

over the old man's shoulder. "Later maybe I'll try some,"
he said. Then Eloise was back and the dog was on Mr.
Tubbs's lap and they were on the way again. The boy supposed that that stop had set some sort of a record as far as
their party was concerned. It couldn't have been much
more than three or four minutes. That suited him just
fine—the shorter, the better.

"What're you eating, Mr. Tubbs?" Spence asked, once
they were a few miles up the Interstate.

"He's not eating," said A. J., "he's chewing. It's tobacco."

"Care for a chaw, missy?"

"What's it taste like?"

"I'd be hard put to explain. It's somethin' you got to
learn for yourself."

"I hear it's like licorice, only more so," said A. J.

"Okay," she said, "I'm game."

Mr. Tubbs held the Beechnut package, its top open, toward the girl and she pinched some of it with her fingers and
tentatively slipped it into her mouth.

"How do you like it?" A. J. asked, leaning forward.

"Too soon to tell."

Suddenly Gwendolyn raised her head from Mr. Tubbs's
lap, pointed her nose to the car's ceiling, and howled.
"Ahoouu," she said, "ahoouu." It was about as mournful a
sound as A. J. had ever heard.

"Oh, oh," said Spence. "A siren. Gwendolyn has very
sensitive ears. She always howls at sirens." She looked up
into the rearview mirror just as A. J. turned to look
through the back window. There were flashing red lights
behind them and they were coming up fast.

"What'll I do?" she asked, chewing furiously on the
tobacco.

"Well, it's a cinch you can't outrace them," A. J. said,

"and sure as hell they're not after you to give you a ticket for speeding. Just slow down naturally—don't slam on the brakes—and sort of ease over onto the emergency strip and keep your fingers crossed."

The car slowed and pulled over to the right and came to a stop. Gwendolyn's howling got louder as the siren neared. This time they've got us sure, A. J. thought. They had about run out of luck. The inside of the Volks was filled with the dancing bright red and blue of the flashing lights and suddenly then, the lights and sound passed them.

"Ambulance," said Eloise, loud enough to be heard over Gwendolyn's howling. She sounded relieved. Shifting into first, she checked the rearview mirror and pulled out into the traffic lane again. Gwendolyn planted another juicy kiss on Mr. Tubbs's cheek. "Shoot," he said crossly. "Make her stop doin' that! Gets a man all slobbery." He wiped at his face with his sleeve.

A. J. let out a deep breath. "That was a close one," he said. "Figured they had us sure, that time. I'd better keep a closer watch behind." And then he realized that it really didn't matter, because if the cops started chasing that little white Volkswagen, it would be no contest at all. And there certainly weren't many places they could pull off to hide along the Interstate.

Mr. Tubbs asked A. J. for the road map and he handed it to him. Then he asked Spence if she had an electric torch in the car. "He means a flashlight," explained A. J.

"I know he means a flashlight," the girl said. She leaned forward and removed an old, battered light from beneath the dashboard and gave it to the old man. Mr. Tubbs unfolded the map and studied it under the weak beam of the flashlight.

"Two ways to get to Flagstaff," he said after a while. "This here road we're on is one way, an' goin' through

Prescott is the other. Me—I'd admire to go through Prescott.''

"How much longer is it that way?" asked Spence.

"Not more'n a few miles," the old cowboy said.

"I vote No," said A. J. "After all, the important thing is for us to get Mr. Tubbs up to his old ranch so he can have a look at it, then get us all back down to Tucson. I think we should go the most direct route."

"What's in Prescott that makes you want to go that way?" the girl asked, ignoring A. J.

"Memories, mostly," said the cowboy. "Used to get down to Prescott now and again. Tolerable town—clean, wide streets, plenty of saloons along Whiskey Row, nice park 'round the courthouse where a man can sit of a warm afternoon and talk with his friends. Least, that's how it used to be. Anymore, I don't know. I'd just admire to see it."

"What do you mean, anymore you don't know?"

"Last time I was in Prescott we was merely passin' through. Mr. Pfeffer, he had an errand there when he was takin' me on down to the rest home. 'Fore that, hadn't been there in quite a long spell. Used to be, though, us boys would head down to Prescott whenever we could string a couple days together. Of a Saturday night we'd go into Flagstaff, it bein' closer, but for special occasions we'd ride on into Prescott.

"Last few years 'fore the ranch got sold, the boys— they'd leave me behind. They was a young bunch an' they'd pile into the pickup and drive on down, sayin' I slowed 'em up, cramped their style. 'Course, they was right. I weren't good for much hell-raisin' once I turned eighty-five."

"Do cowboys really go into town and whoop it up on Saturday nights?" asked A. J. "I thought that was only in the movies."

Mr. Tubbs laughed. "Shoot, we didn't go 'round firin' off our six-guns, like in them movin' picture shows, but Saturday nights was always a big time. Why, we'd drink and carouse and dance with the ladies and we'd get into some mischief if we wasn't careful, an' plenty o' times we *wasn't* careful. Yup, we sure had us a time, them Saturday nights."

"Dancing? Somehow I can't imagine you dancing, Mr. Tubbs," said A. J.

"In my day, sonny, I could keep up with the best of 'em, make no mistake about that." Sonny again. A. J. wished he wouldn't call him that. Or kid. From the back seat the boy could see the old man's hand moving, stroking Gwendolyn. The dog yawned and made a happy squealing, purring sound, almost as if she needed a lube job.

"And of all the places I spent a Saturday night, the Palace Saloon in Prescott was the finest," Mr. Tubbs continued. "Why, the music there—the Professor himself on the piano and another fella playin' the fiddle—was as good as any you'd hear in Paris, France, 'less I miss my guess. An' them ladies, they was as pretty as any you'd find anywhere, an' that good whiskey—it just flowed and flowed, long as a man had the money to pay for it. Yes sir, Prescott. Unless you seen Prescott, you ain't seen nothin', you ain't been nowhere."

"I guess," said A. J., "that means we're going to Prescott."

Gwendolyn climbed up so her head showed over the rear of the front seats, and with her muzzle resting there, a big paw on either side of it and her floppy ears dangling every which way, she stared at A. J. At least he supposed she was staring at him. In the dark car and with his eyes being the way they were, A. J. couldn't quite be sure. Bassets had to be the saddest looking dogs there were, he decided. A. J.

imagined she was sympathizing with him for having to make that long trip when he really didn't want to. Good dog, that Gwendolyn. Smart. If only she didn't have to widdle all the time. But at least she didn't get carsick the way his mother's poodle always did. He hated his mother's poodle.

Then Mr. Tubbs cranked down the window. The blast of air was cold, but it was fresh and it felt good. The old man leaned over and stuck his head out the window and got rid of the tobacco juice. For a second A. J. thought he felt the spray, but he couldn't be sure. That would be too much. He decided he *hadn't* felt the spray and tried not to think about it. Gwendolyn climbed over the old man and stuck her head outside through the open window and her ears flapped in the breeze.

"What did you just do, Mr. Tubbs?" asked Spence. She sounded worried.

"He got rid of the tobacco juice," A. J. said.

"That's what I thought he did," the girl said. "Is that what you're supposed to do with it? Spit it out, I mean?"

"'Course," said Mr. Tubbs. A. J. thought he detected a note of amusement in the old man's voice.

"I didn't know that's what you're supposed to do," Eloise said. "I swallowed mine—back when the ambulance went by. I think I'm going to be sick."

"Well, for Pete's sake, don't be sick in the car," said A. J., "and don't open your window if you have to throw up. Tobacco juice's bad enough!" He closed his left eye and had a look around outside. There was no place to pull off the road—except for the emergency parking, of course—but there were lights up in the distance, and then he saw a sign for the Black Canyon City turnoff. "Can you stick it out a couple of minutes?" he asked her. "There's a turnoff up ahead."

"I think so," she said. She did. The Volkswagen pulled off at the exit and onto the main street. It wasn't much to get excited about. Post office, a few restaurants, an old hotel, some stores, a couple of bars, and everything locked up tight for the night. Maybe even forever. They pulled into a parking lot in front of a dumpy-looking drive-in cafe that was dark inside, like everything else in town, and Eloise hurried out of the car. She stood with her hand on the open door, her head bowed.

"You going to throw up?" A. J. called to her.

"I don't know," she answered. "My stomach hasn't decided yet." For three or maybe four minutes the girl stood waiting. Putting the leash on the dog, the old man let Gwendolyn jump down to the ground, then he followed her, kicking one of his high-heeled boots out of the car. Stooping, he retrieved it, brushed the parking lot dirt from it, then placed it on the floor of the car where it had been, beside the other boot and the bedroll.

"Fetch me the animal's bowl," he called to A. J., "and I'll find us some water." The boy pushed past the saddle and piled out of the car, following the old man and the dog around the side of the building. There was a spigot there and the cowboy filled the dog's dish with water and placed it on the ground for her. Gwendolyn lapped eagerly at it and Mr. Tubbs, the leash looped around his wrist, hunkered and drank at the faucet from his cupped hands. When he was done, A. J. did the same. The water was cold and it tasted good. He let it run into his cupped hands then and he splashed it onto his face and scrubbed with his fingers and palms.

"How you feeling?" A. J. asked Spence when he returned to the car.

"Better, I think. I guess my stomach decided not to throw up, after all."

"There's water over there," he told her. She followed him and he turned on the faucet for her and she drank and rinsed off her face.

Mr. Tubbs and Gwendolyn were waiting for them back at the car. He was seated on a step in front of the drive-in cafe and the dog was on her back, tail wagging, having her belly scratched.

"We're both of us ready when you are," the old man said.

"I'm sorry, but I don't think I can drive any farther right now," Eloise said. "My stomach's better, but my eyes all of a sudden feel like somebody's shoveled sand into them. I just can't keep them open another minute. I'm sorry, I really am."

The idea didn't appeal a whole lot to A. J., but there wasn't much else they could do. He couldn't drive—not without both contacts—and he wasn't about to suggest that the old man take the wheel. That left Gwendolyn. So they climbed back into the car, rolled up the windows, and locked the doors and tried to sleep. A. J. didn't like parking in a strange town at night and everybody going to sleep. No telling *who* might come along and do no telling *what* to them. You read a lot about that sort of thing in the papers.

So A. J. decided to keep watch. He chuckled softly to himself. The old man would get a kick out of that, because in the Westerns, one of the cowboys always stayed awake to keep watch. That's when everything bad always happened. But with Alfie the Kid on guard they were all safe. With index finger and thumb he made a six-gun of his hand and blasted away at the rustlers trying to sneak up on their camp. When he tired of the play he amused himself by listening to the drone of the traffic on the Interstate, which wasn't far from where they were parked. He wished they were up there on the highway, too, but buzzing along south,

toward Tucson, instead of north, toward Flagstaff. And Prescott now, too. Tubbs and the pooch were snoring, but not a sound came from Spence. Either she was still awake or she didn't snore when she slept. He hoped that was the case; the idea of girls snoring was disgusting.

It was lonesome duty, keeping watch. He listened to the Interstate traffic some more and it was a lullaby. Before long the cowboy in the back seat—Alfie the Kid, the one on watch—dropped off to sleep, too.

It was the rocking of the car that awakened A. J. For a moment, with his head heavy with sleep, he thought it was a dream, but saddles didn't reach out and jab your ribs in dreams, and your head didn't bang against car windows in dreams, either. Opening his eyes he glanced quickly around the darkened auto. All at once the rocking stopped and a flashlight beam cut through the darkness of the VW's interior. The light was coming through the window from outside the car. Closing one eye, A. J. saw a face outside the window on Mr. Tubbs's side and another—its nose flattened against the glass—on the girl's side of the car.

Spence awakened, screaming. Growling first, Gwendolyn broke into a deep, angry barking. Mr. Tubbs jumped in his seat.

"What in the hell——" he began.

But the jarring sound of a booted foot kicking the car door on his side silenced him.

"Open up!" came a muffled shout from outside.

"Start the car!" A. J. called. "Jam it into reverse." But his warning was a whisper, and the whisper was too late because Eloise had unlocked the door and someone outside jerked it open.

Suddenly A. J. felt his whole body go weak, and his heart was beating hard and he was trembling all over, even worse than Buck's shaky hands.

11

They must have wheeled the motorcycles up close instead of riding them, because otherwise, there was no way he wouldn't have heard the motors. Surely he couldn't have been sleeping *that* soundly. Not while he was on watch, at least. They were parked not many feet behind the Volkswagen. There were two choppers and a rider for each. Dark as it was, A. J. could see that each rider looked meaner than the other.

One of them held a flashlight that he kept beamed on them. They had made Spence and him climb out of the car and the girl had scooped Gwendolyn into her arms and was holding her. The second rider—the smaller, bearded

one—walked around the car and banged on the door, right next to Mr. Tubbs.

"Leave him be," A. J. called out. The sound of his voice startled him. "He's an old man—he's a hundred!"

"Bullshit!" said the big one, who held the light. "Drag 'im out here, Babe, so's we can keep an eye on him!"

"What are you going to do to us?" asked Spence.

"Never can tell, little lady," the big one said, chuckling. "That Babe there—sometimes he gets weird ideas in his head." He walked the few steps to where the girl stood and then reached a hand out toward her hair. There was a growl deep in Gwendolyn's throat and she snapped at the motorcyclist's hand. Swearing, he drew it back quickly.

In the pale light A. J. could see that the one with the flashlight had short hair and a round, clean-shaven face. He wore a white T-shirt and a blue-jean jacket with its sleeves cut out, like a vest. The other car door opened and Mr. Tubbs climbed slowly out and walked around the auto toward the others. The one called Babe prodded him from behind.

"Now easy there, young fella," Mr. Tubbs said. He held the blanket roll under one arm and with the other hand attempted to straighten his hat.

"Get a load of *this* dude," Babe said, pointing toward Mr. Tubbs with a wrench, and the two motorcyclists laughed.

"Them two got any cash?" Babe asked the clean-shaven one when they were done laughing. Babe had long hair held in place by a red bandanna, tied Apache-style.

"How do I know?" said the other. "I ain't looked yet."

"Well then, you check the old man and the kid, and me, I'll take her around back and I'll check *her* out myself!"

"And when *you* finish checking her, I'll check her myself, just to make sure!" Both of them laughed again.

The big one shined his light into Spence's face and she

looked more frightened than anyone A. J. had ever seen in his life. Heavy as the dog was, she hugged Gwendolyn tighter, closer to her, like a teddy bear.

The boy took a step forward. "All we got is a couple of dollars between us, and the old man—he's broke. He lives in a rest home. You're welcome to what we've got," said A. J., "only just take it and leave us alone!" He reached toward a pocket for his wallet.

Babe raised the wrench and shook it toward A. J. "Easy, kid," he said, "move nice and easy like."

A. J. froze. Suddenly the wrench seemed as big as a sledge hammer. He stood motionless, Spence to his left, holding the dog, Mr. Tubbs to his right, and the two motorcyclists directly in front of them, no more than twelve feet away.

"You," said Babe, pointing the wrench at Eloise. "You got that dog on a leash?"

She nodded.

"Then put the mutt down, but hang onto that leash, hear?"

"I hear." Leaning over, she placed Gwendolyn on the ground.

"Now you walk that doggie nice and slow like, see, over to that porch post, and you tie that leash around the post just as—tight—as—you—can. Got that?" Spence nodded.

As she turned, the dog jerked sharply and pulled away from the girl. It was their chance, thought A. J. When Gwendolyn attacks them they could move in on the motorcyclists and——

"Okay, you two," shouted A. J., shaking a finger at the motorcyclists. "You've had it—that dog's trained to kill!"

The two motorcyclists backed up cautiously a few steps, then halted. The one with the flashlight raised his booted foot, ready to kick. Even before the dog reached them she

stopped, lowered her nose to the ground, and sniffed, wagging her tail. She squatted then and widdled, right in front of the two.

Again Babe and his sidekick laughed, as if it was the funniest thing they'd ever seen. "Yeah, I can see that mutt's a real killer—goes right for the throat, don't she." Watching the dog with the flashlight trained on the growing puddle, they laughed more. Smart dog, A. J. thought.

"Hold on there, you polecats!" A. J. jumped. It was Mr. Tubbs hollering. A. J. looked quickly to his right and there stood the old man, holding a six-gun that looked twice the size of the toy one Buck had worn.

Side by side, the two motorcyclists began walking slowly toward Mr. Tubbs, as if stalking a wild animal.

"Freeze!" he ordered. "This here gun is loaded!" There was no nonsense in his voice. With his thumb he cocked the hammer. They froze. A. J. couldn't believe it. It was just like a Western and there he stood, right in the middle of it, as a hundred-year-old John Wayne with a Stetson cock-eyed on his head, drew a bead on a pair of outlaws. Owl-hoots. That's what they called outlaws.

"Well, lookie there at the dude and his popgun," said Babe. "You in your second childhood, grandpa? You hadn't ought to be playing with guns at your age—it's just liable to go off."

"You know what I think, Babe?" said the other. "I think it ain't loaded, and even if it was, that old bastard ain't got the strength to pull the trigger."

Once more the two began edging toward Mr. Tubbs.

"Damn fools!" shouted the old man, and he waved the barrel of the gun, first toward one, then the other. He lowered the barrel slightly toward the ground in front of them and squeezed the trigger.

KABLOOM!!

For an instant the fiery flash that leaped from the gun in Mr. Tubbs's hands lit up Black Canyon City bright as high noon and the report of the explosion bounced back and forth against the nearby buildings. Smoke filled the air and A. J. took a deep breath of it and sneezed. His eyes watered and there was a ringing in his ears.

Whimpering, Gwendolyn ran to where Spence stood and the dog jumped up, placing her front paws on the girl's thighs, almost knocking her to the ground.

"Now you two git!" Mr. Tubbs hollered, waving the huge six-shooter in the air.

Babe and his friend eyed one another, took one more look at the revolver, turned tail, and ran to their choppers. In seconds they were roaring down the street.

Turning to the girl, A. J. touched her lightly on the arm. "Are you okay, Spence?" he asked.

"I guess so," she said weakly. "I was awfully scared, but I'll be okay now."

"I'm *still* scared," the boy admitted. "My knees are shaking like—like—well, they're shaking, believe me." He paused, then asked, "Can you drive?"

"Sure."

"Then we'd better get out of here ourselves," A. J. said. "They probably heard that gunshot all the way to Phoenix." He picked up Mr. Tubbs's bedroll from where he had dropped it and Eloise took hold of the dog's leash and they hurried to the car and climbed in. It wasn't more than a minute before the white VW was back on the Interstate. A. J. looked out through the back window. He didn't know whether he was watching for police cars or motorcyclists or for a posse on horseback. Just then nothing would have surprised him.

Facing forward, he settled down in his seat and sighed. "You aren't supposed to go around shooting people," he

said to the old man. "I mean, this isn't like Tombstone or Dodge City in the 1880s—this is the *New* West." His ears were still ringing and his own voice sounded funny.

"Didn't shoot no people," said Mr. Tubbs. "If I figured to, I would've, but them two sidewinders—they wasn't worth the lead."

"I didn't think cowboys really carried guns," Spence said. Her voice still sounded weak. "I read an article somewhere that said they didn't—that it was just part of the myth of the Old West."

"Shoot, missy, all us boys carried guns. Maybe not on our hip in a fancy holster like Bucky boy, but at least stuck into our jeans or in a mackinaw pocket or maybe just kep' handy in a bedroll."

"Like tonight? It was in your bedroll?" the girl asked.

"Yup. A feller needed a gun, what with snakes and big cats and all them critters out there."

"Did you ever shoot a—man?" she wanted to know.

"Never did. Never so much as had cause to draw on a two-legged varmint. Not 'fore now, leastways."

"How long has it been since you fired that thing?" asked the boy.

Mr. Tubbs went, "Tsk," as if in deep thought, then answered. "Been the better part o' forty years, I reckon. Thirty-five, least."

"Why, it could have exploded right in your face," said A. J.

"Yup, could've, but it didn't. Sometimes a man has got to take a chance. 'Course, I keep that ol' gun cleaned reg'lar."

"Do the nurses know you have it?" Spence asked.

"Don't reckon so. Them busy-body women—they'd take it away from me quicker'n anything, an' I wouldn't hanker for that to happen. I keep it hid."

There was little traffic on the highway now, with only an

occasional car headed south in the lane beyond the median, and as far ahead as A. J. could see with his weak eyes, there was no sign of the tail lights of another northbound auto. Off to the east the sky was paling. It would be daylight in another hour or so.

"Been thinkin', you young'uns," Mr. Tubbs told them. "What just happened back there—that worries me."

"Worries me, too," A. J. agreed.

"I figure maybe this is a damnfool thing I got you into," said the old cowboy. "Why, if somethin' bad was to happen to one of you young'uns, I'd feel awful sorry. Way I see it, it ain't worth takin' no chances, just to haul me up to see that ol' place.

"Shoot, I seed it plenty when I was ridin' that range country. Ain't no need for me to see it again. I reckon I can die just as happy if we turn around and drive back home, as if we'd keep headin' up north."

"Oh, Mr. Tubbs!" Spence said.

A. J. could hardly believe what he was hearing. It was like a miracle. "Do you really mean that?" he asked eagerly.

"Wouldn't 've said it if I didn't," the old cowboy answered.

For nearly a minute, A. J. thought about it. Finally he shook his head and groaned. "Aw, cripes," he said. "Two or three hours ago I'd have said great, let's turn back, but now we've gone this far, we might as well go on all the way. I mean, if we turned back now, we'd always be sorry about it—sorry that we didn't get you up there to the ranch— sorry that *we* didn't get to see it, either."

"I'm glad you feel that way," Spence told him.

"I honestly don't know *how* I feel," he answered. "I mean, my good sense tells me we should turn around and go home, but at the same time I guess that since we started this

stupid trip, we might as well go ahead and finish it. I can't see how I can be in any more trouble with my folks than I already am, so let's go ahead!''

It was then that the thought came to A. J. that he was beginning to enjoy—well, *almost* enjoy—the whole stupid trip, though he wasn't about to admit it. Not just then, at least. Mr. Tubbs was turning out to be a pretty nice guy after all, except that he was so old, and *that* still bothered A. J. And the way the old cowboy had handled things in Black Canyon City was pretty amazing. Laughing to himself, he realized that he had witnessed something that might've happened a hundred years ago in the Wild West, and he wondered how things might've gone—what might've happened—if the old cowboy hadn't pulled the trigger on those motorcycle outlaws. When he thought of that, he shuddered.

Shifting in his seat to find a comfortable position, he let his hand rest on the saddle, and without thinking, he gave it a few pats. Right now he was drowsy and he decided he'd sleep a little more before they got to Prescott. Who knows, maybe I'll call my parents from Prescott so they won't be worrying, he thought. That would be the practical thing to do. But maybe I won't. He smiled and settled back and dropped off to sleep.

12

They ate breakfast in a cafe in Cordes Junction, where they left the Interstate and got onto the road to Prescott. Past the junction, State Highway 69 began to climb easily toward the distant mountains. The road took them through several small communities strung out along both sides of the highway and past unpaved roads that led to far-off farm and ranch buildings. In time, A. J. told Spence to shift down to third gear again and the old Volkswagen spurted on ahead. Mr. Tubbs took off his Stetson and brushed dust from it with his hand, then carefully straightened the hat on his head. He was getting excited, A. J. noticed.

"We're gettin' there, young'uns," the old man said. "Time was I knowed boys who rode for most of these outfits we're seein' along here. Yes, indeedy," he added, almost to himself.

Then they were passing through different kinds of vegetation than what had been growing in the lower desert lands. Scrub oak? wondered A. J. Or juniper, maybe? Sometime in the past, on an earlier trip to the high country of northern Arizona, they had been pointed out to him, but at the time he hadn't seen much sense in cluttering his mind with things like names of trees. Now he wished that he had listened and remembered. Maybe when he got back home he could find a book about trees of the Southwest and look them up. He thought about asking Spence, or even Mr. Tubbs, what kinds of trees they were, but he was afraid they would think he was dumb if he did, so he didn't ask them.

They passed some "Cold Beer & Pop" places along the road and then a frontier-style shopping center with several stores in it. Civilization. The hills that rose on either side of the highway were more rugged now, and were rocky. Must've played hell carving a road through here, A. J. realized. The VW lost steam and Spence shifted down to second.

"She's just over yonder rise," said the old man. This might be his hundredth or whatever birthday today, thought the boy, but at that moment the old cowboy sounded as excited as a seven-year-old kid at recess time.

They topped that last hill and then the old man let out a whoop. "There she be, young'uns! *There's Prescott!*"

A. J. Zander wanted to stand up and cheer, but there wasn't room enough in the back seat of the Volks.

At the edge of town they stopped at a service station, had the gas tank filled and the oil checked—down a quart—and

the windshield cleaned. They all got out of the car to stretch their legs and A. J. went into the mens' room and combed his hair and washed his hands and face. That helped, but he still wished he could step into a shower and stand for an hour and then crawl into bed, between clean, crisp sheets, and then sleep around the clock. But all he had to look forward to was more time curled up in the back seat with that stinking old saddle. He sneezed. Then they were back in the car.

"So where to now?" asked A. J.

"The Palace Saloon," said the old man, smacking his lips.

"You'll have to direct me," Spence told him, and so Mr. Tubbs played navigator. He talked Eloise on down Gurley Street as it dropped south, then had her stay on Gurley when it turned right at the Smoki Museum. A. J. was worried because the Saturday-morning-shopper traffic was heavy, but Spence buzzed them about town with no difficulties.

"Turn here," Mr. Tubbs would say, and, "Bear to the right," and, "Head due north." With every block he became more excited, his head turning every which way to see all there was to see.

"Yonder is the Hassayampa Inn," he said, poking a finger out the open window. "Fanciest place in town, it was. Just like the big city. Went to a dress-up weddin' there once, and near danced my feet off." To hear him talk the place might've been the Taj Mahal. A. J. closed one eye and studied the building through his single contact as they drove past. The Taj Mahal, it wasn't. It was big and boxy and built of dingy red-brown brick, and it had long ago passed its prime. Just like the old cowboy, thought A. J.

Then Mr. Tubbs told Spence to take a right turn on

Montezuma and pull into a parking slot at the curb. "And here we be," he announced, as though he'd discovered the Mississippi, or something.

"*Where* be we?" asked A. J.

"On Whiskey Row—there's the Palace Saloon an' I'm buyin'!"

"What do you mean, you're buying?" asked A. J. "You don't have any money!"

"Shoot," said the old man, patting his middle. "Got plenty of money right here in my money belt. More'n I'll ever spend if I live to be a hundred." Then the old man started laughing. "Shoot," he said, "I reckon I *am* a hundred!" And he laughed some more.

"Your *money* belt?"

"Yup, you don't reckon I'd carry it in my pocket like a gamblin' feller, do you?"

A. J. asked him where he'd gotten the money.

"Saved it. Last many years out to the ranch, well, there weren't a whole lot to spend money on. Some magazines, tobacco, a pitcher show now and again in town, new shirt or Levi's maybe once a year—an' that's about it. So I just saved my pay and the gov'ment, they keep sendin' me a Social Security check once a month, regular as if I was on the payroll."

The boy moved closer to Mr. Tubbs. "How much money do you have?"

"A. J.!" said Eloise. "You don't ask a person a question like that!"

"Got me plenty here. Maybe eight, nine thousand dollars."

"In cash?"

"Yup," said the old man. "Spends easier that way."

"And you mean to say we've been driving around half

the state of Arizona in this old clunker and fighting off motorcycle gangs and everything, *with nine thousand dollars in cash* just hanging around your middle?''

"I reckon that's what I mean to say."

"But you should have all that money in the bank," Spence said.

"Don't trust banks," he told her. "Never have."

"Then you should invest it in stocks—you can talk to my father when we get home. He'd be happy to help you, I know," said A. J. Might even get a commission out of it, the boy thought. Once he'd said it, he was sorry he had. What did the old man need with more money than he already had? If he actually did have that much money in his money belt, it was more than he'd ever be able to spend living in that rest home, even if he lived a hundred *more* years.

"I've heard of money belts," said the girl, "but I didn't know people ever used them anymore. I've never seen one."

Without saying a word Mr. Tubbs unbuttoned his shirt and his long, woolen underwear, then pulled both open. A. J. looked around to make certain no one was watching, then he leaned forward so he could see better. Sure enough. It *was* a money belt. At least, A. J. supposed it was one, but he'd never seen one, either. It was thick and the old man unzipped it and drew a couple of bills from its long pocket. Fifties. "Reckon that'll buy us a round or two of drinks," he said. Then he closed the money belt and rebuttoned his clothes.

The Palace Saloon—the sign said Palace *Bar*—was near the middle of a block that was mostly stores. The boy wondered where it got the name, Whiskey Row. There weren't *that* many bars along the street. Across Montezuma was the old Yavapai County Courthouse, which stands in the

middle of a park, with benches and bushes and tall trees all around it. They climbed out of the car, locked it, and looked around. A. J. was uneasy about the old man carrying all that money, so he moved as close to him as possible. You never know what's going to happen in a strange town like that, he thought.

"Time was there was 'most nothin' *but* saloons along here," Mr. Tubbs told them as he stepped up the curb onto the sidewalk. A. J. looked up and down the street and saw no more than three or four bars. There was a bookstore, too, and a Western-wear shop and an art gallery, a discount clothing store, some cafes, and an old hotel.

The Palace was easily the oldest looking place on the block. Its entrance was set back a little farther than the others along the street. Even though it was early morning, it was open for business. They stepped inside and paused for a few moments until their eyes became accustomed to the darkened interior. A. J. squinted and looked around.

An ornate, old-fashioned, wooden bar took up most of the left side of the place, and just inside, to the right, was a pool table. Two bearded young men in jeans and sandals were shooting a game of eight ball. Beyond the pool table were rows of tables, and over against the wall were several booths. The tables and booths were empty, but a few men perched on stools along the bar. At the rear of the place, to the left, was a stairway that led to a door marked "Office." At the center rear was a bandstand, with stacked speakers and amplifiers, an electric bass, and an electric guitar on it, as well as a set of drums. Above the bandstand was a cloth banner with the name of a local rock group sewn to it. It looked homemade. The old man led the way to a booth and the three settled down.

"How's it look to you?" asked A. J.

"Hard to say right off," answered Mr. Tubbs. " 'Course I remember it as being a mite fancier and some brighter." A. J. looked around the place. It might've been a set for a big-budget cowboy movie. It looked like a hundred saloons he had seen in Westerns. As the barmaid, a woman in her early twenties, approached, A. J. looked up.

"What'll it be, folks?" she said, looking to the boy.

"Round of beers," the old man said, slapping his hand on the table. The barmaid frowned.

"No," said Spence firmly, before the barmaid could speak. "Make that a round of Shirley Temples."

The barmaid looked to the old man. "What's a Shirley Temple?" he asked her.

"A kiddie drink," she said, a disgusted look on her face.

"They're good," Eloise assured Mr. Tubbs. "I always have one when I go someplace with my folks and they have drinks. There's 7-Up in them and some sweet red syrup and you get a cherry and a slice of orange. You'll like it, you really will."

"Okay, lady," said Mr. Tubbs wrinkling his nose. "Bring us a round of them Shirley Temples." He slapped the table again with his palm. The woman rolled her eyes and returned to the bar. A. J. was embarrassed. He hoped the old man would limit his slapping to the table top.

While they waited for their drinks, Mr. Tubbs told of a hot night one long-ago July when a miner who'd had more to drink than he should've, tipped over a kerosene lamp in a Prescott boarding house.

"Touched off a fire, it did, that all but wiped out Whiskey Row," the old cowboy said.

"But do you suppose that closed things down here? Not on your life, it didn't. Why, even before the ruins quit smolderin' them saloonkeepers salvaged what they could of

their wares and fixtures and set up shop 'cross the street in Courthouse Plaza, and did business there until the saloons could be rebuilt.''

As he finished the story the barmaid returned and placed the drinks in front of them. They were pink and frothy and Mr. Tubbs made a face when he saw them. He reached into his pocket and pulled out an old leather coin purse. Unsnapping it, he drew one of his fifty-dollar bills from it, unfolded it, and handed it to the woman.

She whistled, holding it up to examine more carefully in the daylight that spilled in through the open front door. "You got anything smaller than this? We ain't been open long." Mr. Tubbs shook his head. The barmaid looked to A. J., a questioning expression on her face. A. J. sighed.

"Yeah," he said, and the boy reached into his pocket and dropped a couple of singles on her tray.

"That's better," she said, making change.

"You get any riders in here from the ranches out in the hills?" the old man asked the woman.

"Once in a while a few come in," she said. "The boss, he says there used to be a lot of cowboys coming in here regular in the olden days—especially Saturday nights, he says—but anymore, it's mostly the young crowd. You know, a lot of college kids. Hippies, and that."

"Ever hear mention of a Pete Clayton fella comin' 'round?" asked Mr. Tubbs. "Or a curly-headed boy named Britton?"

The barmaid shook her head. "No, those names—they really don't ring a bell with me, but like I said, I'm new." She returned to the bar.

"Used to be they had *gents* workin' behind the bar," said Mr. Tubbs, sounding disgusted. "Big fellas, ever' one of 'em, with white shirts and black bow ties and clean white

aprons, an' wasn't one didn't have a big, wide handlebar moustache. An' my, how they kep' order in this place. Why, a fight would no more'n break out an' them big barkeeps was jumpin' over the bar and wadin' into it, swingin' them billy clubs they kep' handy for just such occasions.

"Some Saturday nights, why, there'd be as many as half a dozen little frays here. Oh, the Palace, it were a fine place in its day."

He took a sip of his Shirley Temple and smacked his lips. "Now *that* tastes right good," he said.

"We're *forgetting!*" Eloise said to A. J., placing a hand on his arm. She raised her glass in the air. "Happy birthday, Mr. Tubbs!" she said. Then she turned to the boy. "A. J.—tell Mr. Tubbs happy birthday!"

"Happy birthday," he said, without much enthusiasm. He looked around to see if anyone was watching, then lifted his Shirley Temple and clinked it against Spence's glass. "You aren't going to sing that dumb song again, are you?" whispered A. J.

But she did. All the way through. A. J. didn't join in, though. By the time she had finished everybody in the Palace was looking at them. The boy was glad it was early morning and the place wasn't crowded.

"Thank you, missy, you make me right proud," said Mr. Tubbs. He took another sip of the drink, then stared into the glass. "You know," he said thoughtfully, "you young'uns are bein' powerful nice to me. Never had nobody to do things for me the way you two are. I want you to know I 'preciate it. Truly, I do."

"Why, Mr. Tubbs, we're enjoying it all ourselves, otherwise we wouldn't have planned this," said Spence. "Isn't that right, A. J.? Aren't we enjoying this trip?"

"Sure," the boy said. "I'm having the time of my life."

"I'm happy to hear that," the old man said, " 'cause I sure wouldn't want to be puttin' you young folks out, none."

"Don't even think of such a thing," the girl said. "It's our pleasure."

"Well, seein' as how you both feel that way, and since we're goin' to be up in Flagstaff anyways, once we leave the ranch there's a fella I'd admire to see there in town. Ol' pal of mine. He's in a home up there. Might be I'd hanker to move up there myself, so I'd have a friend to help pass the time of day."

A. J. let out his breath slowly and slouched down in the booth. "Sure, why not," he said.

The old cowboy brightened. "Ain't seen ol' Arnie in a good long while. Rode together a lot of years, we did, and he's as good a man as ever I saw when it comes to handlin' a rope. A good ol' boy."

"And he lives there in Flagstaff?" asked Eloise.

"Yup, he's in a fine home up there, run by the county. Nice place, in a piney forest out beyond the edge of town. Think I'd enjoy bein' there lots more'n the place I'm in now. The folks there is my kind of folks—not the city kind."

"An' if it don't work out to move, why, it'd just be nice seein' ol' Arnie Spack again. We rode a good many miles together, shared a good many hard times and plenty of laughs."

"We'd miss you if you moved up there, wouldn't we, A. J.?"

"Yeah," the boy said. And then he thought for a moment and he realized that he *would* miss the old man on those Saturday visits to the rest home. "Yeah," he repeated, "I guess we really would."

Standing, A. J. drained his Shirley Temple and clunked

the empty glass on the table. "Come on, you two," he said. "With all we've got planned, we'd better get going." Standing, looking at the others, he wondered if they ever *would* get home.

Mr. Tubbs stood finally and looked around the Palace one more time, eyed the barmaid and the bearded pool players, then shaking his head, left the bar. "Lady barkeeps," he grumbled. Spence and A. J. followed slowly behind the old cowboy.

13

It was even before they reached Jerome that the Volkswagen broke down. After leaving Prescott they had driven north on the main highway and picked up the alternate route a few miles out of town. It took them through some more ranch country and then into an area of hills and interesting rock formations that A. J. supposed must be a resort region because there were a lot of motels and trailer courts and cafes and real estate offices strung along the highway.

The alternate road was narrow and winding for a time and then it straightened out to go through more of those flat, grassy ranchlands. As always in Arizona, there were

mountains off in the distance. Along both sides of the road were some beautiful tiny white wild flowers. A. J. didn't know what kind they were; he'd never been at all interested in wild flowers. Maybe now he'd have to read a book about wild flowers, too. There were clusters of tumbleweed caught on the barbed-wire fences along both sides of the road, and beyond the fences were occasional bunches of cattle, just grazing and taking it easy, which is all A. J. ever saw cows do.

Eloise was barreling right along and the old man must've been feeling good because he started singing an old cowboy song and A. J. was sleeping—at least trying to sleep—curled up with the saddle. Then the road started to climb again.

A. J. could feel the engine begin to labor and without even opening his eyes, he told the girl to shift down. She did. In the back seat the boy swayed, first against the side of the car, then the other way, into the saddle. He opened his eyes and stretched an arm along the back of the rear seat to steady himself. The climb became even greater and Eloise shifted down again, to second, even before A. J. told her to. The road was a snaking thing, with switchbacks and hairpin curves, and A. J. didn't like it. He wasn't at all keen on mountain driving, especially with an inexperienced driver at the wheel of an old rattletrap. At one point he closed his left eye so he could see clearly through the contact, and right away he wished he hadn't. What he saw worried him. There was a sheer drop of several hundred feet to a rocky canyon or gorge or whatever they called it, far below. He clutched the back of the seat even harder.

"This is fun!" said Eloise. "I've never driven in mountains before and I love it!" She flipped the steering wheel to negotiate a sharp curve and A. J. lunged against the saddle.

The engine wasn't sounding right, and A. J. leaned forward. They were on a short level stretch of road now, that led to the next curve and climb. The car should have been gaining speed because it was in second, but it continued to slow down. A. J. glanced at the speedometer; the needle was dropping fast.

"You got it floored?"

"If I had it pushed down any harder my foot would go through the floorboard," she said. "It just seems so sluggish—it's not doing anything!"

"You sure you got plenty of gas?"

"We filled in Prescott and that should get us a long way."

"Don't sound as it should to me, neither," put in the old man. "Somethin's clunkin' an' clankin' up there. Even I can hear it, deef as I am."

A short distance ahead was a small parking area where motorists could pull off to view the scenic sweep of the valley.

"Try to make it to that turnoff up there," A. J. said.

A determined look on her face, Eloise leaned over the wheel and spoke words of encouragement to the VW, as if that would help. "Come on, car, just a little farther," the girl said. Leave it to a girl to think talking to a dumb car would help, thought A. J. It was as silly as people talking to plants. The Volks was barely moving. Eloise eased as close to the edge of the road as possible and finally, as they came to the turnoff, she steered it sharply off the road.

She didn't even have to step on the brake. The car just rolled to a stop and died without so much as a whimper. Spence turned off the ignition and pulled the emergency brake.

"Well," said A. J., "here we are. I hope *you* know something about fixing cars, because it's a cinch I don't!"

"I know where the gas goes," she said, "and that's about all."

"Great," the boy said. "So here we sit, stranded halfway up a mountain in the middle of God-knows-where. We'll be here forever."

"Oh, don't get so dramatic," Spence said. She looked around. "At least the view is nice and besides, somebody'll come along and help us."

"Yeah, like those motorcyclists from Black Canyon City," said A. J.

"Reckon I'll have me a look," said the old man. "I've fixed a flivver or two in my day."

As Mr. Tubbs climbed from the car he gave Gwendolyn's leash a tug. "C'mon, dog," he said. The old man and Gwendolyn were up front by the time A. J. and Spence were out of the auto. The hood was raised and Mr. Tubbs was bent over, peering inside. As they approached he straightened up.

"No wonder you're havin' troubles, missy," the cowboy said. There was a puzzled look on his face. "Somebody clean stole your engine. Ain't no sign of it up here."

A. J. groaned. "That's the trunk," he said. "The motor is in the rear on a VW."

The boy led the others to the back of the car, fiddled with the catch, and lifted the hood. "There," he said, pointing at the engine. "Nobody stole the motor—it's just hiding."

The cowboy bent over, his hands on his legs just above the knees, and he gazed into the engine, as Eloise took the dog's leash from him.

"What does *he* know about VWs?" A. J. asked quietly. "Why, he didn't even know where to find the engine! This is a waste of time. Why don't you get out there and flag down a car? Face it, we need help."

"Let's wait a minute," Eloise said. "Who knows, maybe he *can* do something. It'd make him feel good if he could."

"Lookie here," the old man said brightly. He was pointing inside the engine. A. J. looked but didn't see anything in particular.

"Look at what?"

"Right there," the old man said impatiently. "See where that there carburetor is mounted on the intake manifold? It's come plumb loose. Them little nuts holdin' it together at the flange must've come clear loose and fell off someplace along the line."

Poking his head closer, A. J. closed one eye to peer through his contact. He didn't see an intake manifold or a flange or a carburetor or anything. In fact, he realized he wouldn't have known a flange if it nipped him on the nose. He'd never admit it, though.

"Yeah, I guess you're right," he said finally. "Nuts are gone, all right. Well, I guess that really puts us in quite a pickle."

" 'Pears so," said Mr. Tubbs. He was standing with one arm across his chest, the other hand raised to stroke his chin. He was studying the engine, a frown on his face, and he was gumming his lower lip.

"Think maybe I can fix it," Mr. Tubbs said, raising a bristly eyebrow.

"My father keeps a tool kit in the trunk—I'll get it," Spence said.

"Sonny, you crawl back in that car and fetch me my bedroll."

"This is no time to chew tobacco," the boy argued.

"Ain't about to chew, sonny—just fetch!"

Mr. Tubbs opened the tool kit the girl had brought, and selected a pair of pliers from it.

"This'll do just fine, missy," the old man said, working them open and shut again. When A. J. brought the bedroll,

Mr. Tubbs placed it on the ground and poked his hand into it and rummaged about. What *didn't* the cowboy carry in that blanket roll? wondered A. J.

"There she be," he said finally, a smile lighting his face, and he pulled a snarl of baling wire from within the folds. He held it up for the others to see.

"You mean to say you're going to try to fix that car with a hunk of wire?"

"Not goin' to *try* to fix it, sonny, I'm *goin'* to fix it!" The cowboy sounded awfully sure of himself. Maybe he *could* fix the stupid engine.

"Okay, Mr. Tubbs, you're the boss. What can I do to help?"

"Just you keep out of my hair, sonny," Mr. Tubbs said as he knelt down at the engine. A. J. sighed, stepped back a foot or two, and stared at the engine. It made as much sense to him clear through the contact, as it did blurry with both eyes open.

The carburetor was the thing on top, he supposed, and the intake manifold was what came up from somewhere below to meet it. There were things like collars at the bottom of the carburetor and the top of the manifold, if that's what it was, and he could see where the nuts were missing from the two bolts, which passed loosely through holes in the collars. He was glad he didn't have to write an exam on the engine for general science, or anything. He couldn't imagine why some guys were so anxious to take auto shop at school.

Those little collars probably were what the old man called the flanges. Flange. That was a funny word, A. J. thought, but it was probably as good a name for those collars as anything else. As he watched, the old man poked with the pliers at the carburetor where it had separated from the intake manifold and wiggled it until it settled down

perfectly snug. The bolts—minus their nuts—stuck down slightly through the flanges then. A. J. was proud of himself for being able to figure out what was happening.

When he had the carburetor seated properly, the old man looped the end of the baling wire around the intake manifold and the bolts and then began wrapping the wire round and round, pulling it tighter with each turn. Then he snipped the wire and twisted the two ends together with the pliers. He tapped the carburetor with the pliers then, to make certain it was secure.

"Is that all there is to it?" A. J. asked. "Why, I could've done that myself. It's simple!"

Spence stared at him. "Doing it is one thing," she said, "but knowing *what* to do is something else!" She sounded like a teacher.

"Start 'er up," the old man said to her. Eloise handed the dog's leash to A. J., climbed in, and started the engine. It sputtered, but didn't take hold. "Try 'er again!" Mr. Tubbs shouted.

This time the engine started right away. It sounded good, thought A. J. Better than it had sounded the whole trip. Those bolts must've been awfully loose all along.

"Think that'll hold?" A. J. asked.

"Yup," Mr. Tubbs replied. "She'll hold, an' if she don't, I got more wire." He stuffed what was left of the baling wire back into the bedroll and handed it to A. J. Then, after replacing the tools in the trunk, he had one more look at his handiwork, "Gun 'er," he called to Spence, and she tromped down on the accelerator and the engine purred the way it must've the day it rolled off the assembly line in Germany. Well, almost.

"Where'd you ever learn how to fix a Volkswagen?" Spence asked when they were back in the car. "I didn't think you'd ever even ridden in one before."

"Hadn't," he said, "but a gasoline engine's a gasoline engine. Certain things got to happen inside of one if it's goin' to work. Get right down to it, one motor's 'bout the same as the next, be it from Germany or Detroit or wherever."

"I thought all you knew how to do was rope cows, mend harness, and that sort of thing," said A. J. "I didn't know you were a mechanic, too."

"Surprisin' what a man can do when he's pressed," Mr. Tubbs answered. "If there's a broke' down tin lizzie needs fixin' out to the ranch, a man fixes it. Ain't no garage mechanic to go to. That's the simple fact of it."

The car seemed to be perking right along and that pleased A. J. The sooner they got up to Flagstaff and saw the ranch and visited the old man's friend, the sooner they could head home. They continued to climb and then they were in Jerome, which had been a copper-mining town in years past, but now appeared to be mostly a rundown ghost town that existed on tourist trade, with restaurants and craft shops and little museums tucked away in buildings that clung to mountainsides. A. J. had once heard that the whole town was sliding down the mountain and he could understand why, seeing the way the buildings just hung there. Or maybe it was only the jail that was sliding downhill. He didn't remember for sure. He'd have to look up *that,* too, when he got home. That made trees, wild flowers, and ghost towns. He was going to be busy. But if he was grounded, as he supposed he'd be, he'd have plenty of time for reading.

After slowing to travel the narrow, winding streets of Jerome, it was mostly downhill to Clarkdale and Cottonwood. A. J. tried to keep his eyes open, but he was so sleepy that it was a losing battle. It wasn't until they were approaching Sedona that Spence called to him to wake up.

"Have you ever seen such pretty rocks?" she asked. The

boy opened his eye—the one with the contact—and had a look around. He had to admit that it was something to see, and he wished he had been wearing both contacts. Many of the formations were deep red at the bottom and pushing upward, gave way to rich golden tones in their higher reaches. They were unreal, thought A. J., and looked as though they might've been designed by Walt Disney. Sedona was another tourist town, but it was more crowded than Jerome and it looked a lot higher priced. Traffic moved slowly through the town, past art galleries and fancy restaurants and Indian craft shops and motels and bars. Once out of Sedona, they followed the narrow road as it cut through a forest that had a creek weaving through it. Now and again the creek and road were close enough together that A. J. could see the water from the car. There were picnic tables and recreation areas along the way, and cabins to rent and places to camp. There were a lot of fishermen along the creek's banks.

"Case you're wonderin'," said the old man, "this here is Oak Creek Canyon. As pretty a spot as you'll find on God's earth."

"It's okay, I guess," A. J. said.

They had driven for some distance through the canyon when Eloise pulled over in front of a store that had gas pumps in front of it and off to one side, cabins to rent.

"You figuring on renting a cabin?" A. J. asked her.

"No," she said, "but I'm tired. I want to stretch my legs for a minute." They went into the store and bought some cold drinks and carried the cans across the highway to where the creek ran close to the road. The old man took Gwendolyn's leash and the cowboy and dog walked upstream, to where the trees and shrubs were thicker. A. J. and Spence climbed down the bank to the rushing water and walked a fallen log to a cluster of rocks that was like an

island in the stream. They sat and she pulled off her shoes and rolled up her jeans and let her feet dangle in the water. A. J. reached down and plunged a hand into the water, withdrawing it quickly. "Icy," he said.

"Feels good," she answered, splashing her feet.

"How far is it to Flagstaff?"

"I don't know. Twenty-five miles at most."

"I'm hungry," said A. J. "We haven't eaten since breakfast, and that was ten years ago."

"You had a Shirley Temple and you're having a drink right now," she told him.

"Yeah, but I need something I can sink my teeth into. You can't sink your teeth into a Shirley Temple. My stomach's growling like anything."

"I know," she said. "I can hear it. Well, we can eat a late lunch right after we get back to Flagstaff from the ranch and see Mr. Tubbs's friend."

"And then home?"

She nodded.

"Good," he said. "I hope my folks remember me. It's been so long since they've seen me."

Spence laughed. "How could they ever *forget* you?" she asked, and she kicked a spray of water at him.

"Hey, cut it out," he complained. "I'm cruddy enough without you splashing dirty creek water all over me. Bet it'll take a month of showers to get clean again. I miss it when I can't change my underwear."

Leaning toward him, she sniffed. "So do I," said Spence smiling. "I miss it when you can't change your underwear, too."

He curled a lip and made a face at her.

"Why did you have to say those unpleasant things while Mr. Tubbs was fixing the car?" she asked after a time. "We were in real trouble there and at least *he* could do something about it. You—you were totally helpless."

"I don't know," the boy said thoughtfully. "It's not like I mean it, or anything, but I open my mouth and those words just come out. Funny thing, I'm even beginning to like him."

"You have a funny way of showing it."

"I know—I'm a million laughs," A. J. said.

"Are you jealous of him, or is it just because he's old that makes you act that way?" Spence asked.

"I wish I knew," he said. "Maybe subconsciously I don't want to get too buddy-buddy with him—involved, like you said before—for fear he'll up and die on me, the way Mrs. Koplin did."

"But you can't act like that toward every old person you ever meet. Besides, you're going to be old some day, yourself, A. J., and you might not like the idea, but you're going to die. Is that part of it, A. J.? Are you afraid of getting old and dying?"

"I told you, I'm not going to get old," he said. "I decided—I'm going to find the Fountain of Youth."

"I'm serious, A. J. If you go through life avoiding old people, you're going to miss an awful lot. They have so much to offer us—so much experience to pass along to us. If you keep turning your back on old people just because Mrs. Koplin disappointed you by dying—well, you'll be the loser. Of course she died, everybody does," said the girl.

"You might find the Fountain of Youth for yourself, but your mother and father are going to get old and so are my folks and I'm going to get old and——"

"Okay, I get the picture. Probably you're right, but I've felt this way for so long that I can't help it. I do feel better about it, though, since I told you about Mrs. Koplin. Like I said, I'm even getting to where I sort of like Mr. Tubbs. I'm trying, believe me."

"Then try harder."

"You make that sound like an order."

"What if I say please."

"Say it."

"Please."

"Okay," he said. "I'll be so disgustingly sweet you'll want to throw up."

It was cool and the splashing sound of the water was soothing. "You know, A. J., I like you, I really do," said the girl. "Sometimes you act like you're cynical and mean—especially to Mr. Tubbs—but underneath it all I think there's a really nice person."

"Don't be silly," he said.

"I'm not being silly, I mean it. You've got good instincts, A. J., and they've been showing more and more since I met you. You've been sort of a closet human being and finally you're beginning to come out of the closet—the good in you is beginning to show."

"That's your imagination. I'm nasty to the core."

"Oh, come off it. How many guys would do what you're doing? I mean, would do this for some old man they didn't even really know, the way you're doing?"

"Like I'm doing? Nuts. I'm not doing anything. You're doing the driving, the old man is protecting us with his gun and he's fixing the car—me? I'm not doing anything. I'm just along for the ride. The spare tire—that's me."

"You never know when you'll need a spare tire," she said, reaching out and touching his arm. "And it's always a comfort to know you have one."

The boy felt his cheeks flush. If only she weren't so old, he thought. Almost eighteen. She's old enough to be my big sister! Well, *almost*.

"Okay," said Spence. "I guess we'd better get going."

A. J. scurried up the bank, then turned to give her a hand. For a few moments they stood looking at one another, their hands still clasped. The boy closed that one eye so he could see her more clearly.

"You know," he said, "something the old man said sort of bothered me."

"What's that, A. J.?"

"He said that until this morning, when you kissed him happy birthday, he'd never been kissed by a girl with a mouthful of barbed wire."

"So?"

"So I haven't, either."

She grinned. "Well, you aren't as old as he is." There was a teasing tone in her voice.

"I know, but I don't want to have to wait until I'm a hundred before I try it."

"Who knows," she said, giving his hand a squeeze. "Maybe you won't have to." And then she turned and hurried toward the car.

14

A. J. Zander IV closed one eye and studied his face in the mirror of the filling station restroom, and he wasn't pleased with what he saw. He really looked cruddy. Why, he hadn't shaved in two—or maybe it was three, now—days. The boy laughed to himself. He only shaved once a week, anyway, and usually it was hard to tell, just looking at his chin, whether it was the day before or the day after his Saturday shave.

No matter how you figured it, shave or no, he looked lousy. His mother would have a fit if she saw him now. He

washed his hands and sloshed water on his face and then tried to restore order to his unruly hair, for all the good it did. He wished he had thought to bring his toothbrush with him, because his teeth were coated thick with crud and his mouth tasted as though something had crawled into it and died there.

Stepping outside, he hung the key on the hook in the office, then walked out to the gas pumps where the VW was parked.

"Got something back here in the engine I'd like you to take a look at," he told the attendant. He led the way to the back of the car and raised the hood.

"See there, where the wire's holding that whatchamacall-it? You think it'll hold for a while?"

The attendant squatted down and tapped the carburetor with his tire gauge. "It's solid," he said. "That'll hold easy until you can get it fixed right at a VW garage where they have all them metric tools."

"But it's okay to drive, maybe three hundred miles?"

"No sweat," the attendant assured him. "Whoever done that knew what he was doing. It's as good a piece of make-do mechanics as I've seen for a while." Then he stood and looked at A. J. "That'll be five and a quarter, including the oil."

"Collect from the old guy, he's loaded."

The attendant shook his head. "He tried to pay me, but all he's got is a fifty and I sure can't change that. He said to collect from you."

Reaching for his wallet, the boy muttered under his breath. Mr. Tubbs was in his seat in the car and Spence was still in the women's restroom. He climbed into the car and settled down beside the saddle. It still smelled as bad as it had at first. A. J. sneezed.

"Bless you, sonny. You takin' cold?"

"No," said the boy. "It's this saddle. I think I'm allergic to it. Horses make me sneeze, too."

The old man laughed. "Lucky thing you never took up cowboyin', sonny. You'd 've had the miseries the live-long day." Despite himself, A. J. laughed, too.

"Yeah, I can just see myself sitting on top of a horse at roundup time, sneezing my dumb head off and blowing my nose while the other guys did all the work." He wondered if John Wayne was allergic to horses.

"'Fraid you wouldn't 've lasted long," Mr. Tubbs said. Then Eloise was back in the car and as they were pulling out of the service station driveway, Mr. Tubbs began giving her directions. He was a great one at giving directions.

Flagstaff was larger and more sprawling than A. J. had supposed it would be, and it was mostly hotels and motels, franchise restaurants, gas stations, and curio shops. A real tourist town. And he saw more Indians than he had ever seen before in his life. He asked Mr. Tubbs about them.

"Them are mostly Navvy-hos," the old cowboy said. "Few Hopis, too. The Navvy-hos—they got them their big reservation not far from here. Come in to town here to trade and shop."

For a while A. J. was convinced that the old man was lost. He had them going one way and then another through town and the boy had no idea in which direction they were headed. But he got them onto a road that took them past houses and some scattered business places and then gradually left the city behind. Maybe he knew where he was taking them after all. Presently Mr. Tubbs began humming.

A. J. didn't know the name of the song, but the tune was familiar. It was one of those hokey cowboy ballads that go on and on forever, getting sadder by the verse. But the old man seemed anything but sad. In fact, the longer he hummed, the happier he seemed.

The boy could understand why; after all, Mr. Tubbs was going home. It was peculiar, though. He wasn't going home to some*body*—to a sister or mother or even a close friend. He was going home to a place, to a place where he had spent most of his life. A. J. couldn't think of any place he had ever lived or even just visited, that would get him so excited.

"Many's the time we traveled this road, young'uns, goin' into town for some Saturday night funnin', then headin' back of a Sunday mornin', more dead than alive, for all the *hoo*rahin' we'd done. My," he said, shaking his head, "my, but wasn't them the days."

"Oh, they must've been wonderful days, Mr. Tubbs," said Spence.

"Many's the Saturday night I blew a full month's pay in town. 'Course, that was when I was a young sprout an' didn't know no better. Once I got older and got my sensibles, I didn't try to drink them saloons dry."

And then the old man fell silent, scratching Gwendolyn behind her ears and studying the country they were driving through. They passed along a stretch of mountain road with plenty of curves, and A. J. clung to the saddle's pommel to keep his balance. Presently the land leveled and Spence shifted back into fourth gear.

"Lookie there," said Mr. Tubbs, pointing off to the left. A. J. looked, but all he saw was some cows. "Them's Herefords in that bunch. Some fine stock. Yessiree bob, some fine stock."

Gwendolyn stirred, stretched, and sat up on the old man's lap. She lifted a paw and scratched at the window. As Eloise began to slow the car, Mr. Tubbs spoke. "If you reckon she can hold off, just drive on, missy. Road into the Pfeffer place is less'n a mile farther."

"I'm willing to chance it if you are," she answered, and

she stepped down on the accelerator, giving the VW a new spurt of energy. Mr. Tubbs wriggled uncomfortably in his seat.

"Well, it's sure about time," said A. J., yawning. "I never thought we'd get here."

The asphalt road ribboned through the gently rolling hills of the rich grassland country. Off in the distance, A. J. could see weathered ranch buildings here and there, and in almost every direction there were far-off mountains.

"Just beyond the next hill," said Mr. Tubbs, "and I'm home!" With both hands he reached up and straightened his Stetson, tugging it firmly on his head. They topped the hill and the old man looked about and sucked in his breath sharply.

"Shoot," he said softly.

"What is it?" asked Spence, pumping the brake pedal. "Is something wrong?"

"Shoot," the old man said again. "Ever'thing is wrong. Just lookie yonder—see for yourself!"

Up ahead where the old man was pointing, was a billboard, set in an open field a hundred feet back from the highway.

"Choice Lots Still Available," said the billboard. "HAPPY HACIENDA RANCH ESTATES—Own Your Own One-Acre Ranchette in Arizona's Beautiful Cattle Country." In one corner of the sign was a cartoon drawing of a huge cowboy boot with a spur on it.

Beside the sign was a dirt road that angled off to the right and disappeared beyond a hill. Across the dirt road was a small wooden building, constructed to resemble a frontier saloon, complete with a high false front. Atop the building was another sign that said, "HAPPY HACIENDA RANCH ESTATES—Sales Office," and on the door a smaller sign invited, "Howdy, Mosey In." A. J. groaned.

"Cripes," he said to no one in particular, "how cornball can they get?"

"This is it?" Eloise asked Mr. Tubbs. "This is where you worked all those years?" She stopped the auto on the road.

Slowly he nodded his head.

"Maybe we should just turn around and head back to town," the girl suggested. Mr. Tubbs didn't answer and she repeated it in a louder voice.

"Nope," he said. "I want to see the old place. Might be they ain't touched it yet. Maybe they're just leavin' the buildin's as they was."

Spence nosed the car off the pavement onto the dirt road. As the VW began to move forward a man stepped from the sales office and hurried their way. He raised a hand to halt them.

Through his contact A. J. could see that the man was fat, was in his forties or maybe fifties, and was wearing a big white cowboy hat that looked as if it had come from the dime store. His cowboy shirt was purple silk with orange roses on it, and his belly hung over the low-slung frontier pants. If he was wearing a belt, his belly hid it. The man hobbled along in new-looking cowboy boots, as though his feet hurt him, like ol' Buck.

Spence rolled down the window as he approached. "Howdy, neighbors," he said. "Welcome to Happy Hacienda Ranch Estates!" He leaned over to look into the car, placing his hands against the door. "You folks interested in our fine property here?"

"Not really," said A. J. from the back seat. "We're just sort of looking around."

"Glad you stopped by. Models of our two- and three-bedroom ranch homes are on up the road a piece. Drive on and have a look at 'em, if you care to. They're going fast, I tell you. Why, even though this is Saturday afternoon, we

have a work crew on the job. Here's a brochure and my card—Crawford's the name—and if you have any questions, drop by here and I'll be happy to answer 'em for you.''

A. J. reached out and took the brochure and then Spence stepped down on the gas pedal. The salesman moved back from the car as it pulled away. A. J. chuckled to himself about the look on the guy's face. Disgusted, really, because if there was anything their little group didn't look like, it was prospective ranchette buyers. They rolled along the dirt road, raising a cloud of dust behind them. A. J. had to hurry, glancing first to the left, then to the right, to read all the little signs placed along the sides of the road. They were in the same shape as the cartoon boot on the big billboard. "Sewers In,'' announced one, and another said, "Low Down Payment.'' And other signs read: "Sidewalks'' and "Solid Investment'' and "Water'' and "Paved Streets'' and "Small Monthly Payment'' and "Easy Financing'' and "Electricity.''

At the top of a hill, Mr. Tubbs told Eloise to pull over and stop. Holding the leash, he let the dog jump to the ground, then climbed stiffly from the auto. Spence and A. J. followed. Out beyond them were the model homes of Happy Hacienda Ranch Estates, each on its one-acre lot. The homes were of concrete block, one painted pink and the other an earthy beige, both with bright-colored wood trim and plenty of fancy gingerbread. The houses were festooned with strings of plastic pennants, and looked about as much like ranch houses as igloos do, thought A. J. Other houses were under construction, and although it was Saturday afternoon, the construction men were on the job, just as the salesman had said. Business must be good at Happy Hacienda, the boy supposed. There was the hollow thunking sound of hammering and the whine of electric saws

cutting boards. A fork lift was unloading piled blocks from a truck, and two pre-mix concrete trucks awaited their turns to dump their loads. Farther on, a bulldozer leveled a hill.

For what must've been five minutes, Mr. Tubbs stood on the rise looking down silently at the construction activity. A. J. and Spence were nearby with Gwendolyn. None spoke until the old man did.

"Over yonder, where that yella truck sits—that were the main house. That's where the Pfeffers lived. Weren't hardly what you'd call a fancy showplace fit for royalty, but it was a fine house, just as solid built and comfortable as any you'd find anywhere." His voice was quieter than A. J. had heard it since he'd met him, and A. J. was afraid the old man was going to start bawling.

Turning slightly and pointing his finger at a pile of raw earth to the left of the yellow truck, he continued. "There sat the bunkhouse, where me'n the boys done our sleepin'. Just a plank place, it was, with a pot belly stove, but it was snug an' cozy warm in the wintertime. We had us double bunks in there and a few tables for writin' and playin' cards, an' there was some chairs. My bunk was a bottom one over in the far corner, and there I slep' away 'most a lifetime." The old man pulled a wrinkled red bandanna from a hip pocket and blew his nose.

"An' over to the left, 'bout where that pinky house stands, was the barn, and just short of it was the corral. Rough pine logs, it was, and sturdy. We kep' our workin' string of horses in the corral so's we wouldn't have to chase 'em of a cold mornin', an' the other horses grazed the grasslands, as did the cows."

A chilling wind gust blew up the hillside and A. J. zipped his jacket and studied the old man.

With a broad sweep of his arm, the cowboy spoke of pastures that stretched as far as the eye could see. "And

our summer range," he said, "was in the high meadows of them yonder mountains."

Quietly the three stood looking out across the broad expanse of grazing land. Gwendolyn had stretched out in the afternoon sun. All that looking—not wanting to miss anything the old man was pointing at—hurt A. J.'s eyes and he closed them for a few moments and tried to visualize what the place must have looked like.

"But it's all gone, now," said Mr. Tubbs. "It's changed. Ain't nothin' the same, 'cept the mountains an' the sky."

"In time everything changes, Mr. Tubbs," Spence said.

"She's right. Nothing ever stays the same," said the boy.

"It appears tomorrow has done caught up with me," the old man said, "an' they've bulldozed under all my yesterdays."

Mr. Tubbs turned and walked the few steps to the side of the road and slowly hunkered. Gwendolyn wagged her tail and tugged at the leash to get over beside him. Eloise followed the dog. Gwendolyn placed a front paw on the old man's knee and raised her wrinkled basset face to him. He reached down and scratched her head and behind her ears, then patted her a few times on the side, as if to dismiss her. Spence tugged gently on the leash and the dog went to her.

Reaching down, Mr. Tubbs scooped a handful of earth and closed his fist around it. Slowly, he stood then and A. J. saw that he brought his closed hand to his chest, as if it held gold or diamonds or something valuable, instead of just dirt.

The old man began humming a mournful tune—quietly at first, then louder—as he stood, gazing out at the distant mountains where Pfeffer cattle had browsed in the summers of years past.

A. J. looked at Spence and saw that she had a thoughtful, faraway look on her face, and he wanted to say something to her to break the uncomfortable silence, or something to cheer up Mr. Tubbs, but then he realized that that wasn't

the time to speak. He looked at the old man's closed hand and realized then that the earth it held *was* a treasure to him; to Mr. Tubbs it was far more valuable than a handful of gold or even diamonds.

Abruptly then, as if he had made a decision, the old cowboy quit his mournful humming. He opened his hand and stared down at the dirt it held, then let it filter through his fingers to the ground. Wiping his hand on the leg of his Levi's, he turned to the others.

"An' now, sonny, I'd be beholden to you if you'd fetch my saddle," said the old man. His voice was quieter than A. J. had heard it before.

"But there're no horses here for you to ride," the boy protested.

"It makes no nevermind, sonny, just fetch it, if you please."

A. J. went to the VW, opened the door, pushed the seat forward, and tugged the saddle free. He carried it to the old man and dropped it to the ground at his feet. Then he sneezed.

"What are you going to do with the saddle?" asked A. J.

"Get shut of it," said the cowboy. "It's plain to see I've done my ridin'."

"But you can't just leave your saddle out here," Spence said. "I mean, you've had it so long. It's like—well, it's like the saddle's a part of you, like your arm or your leg or——"

"She's right," broke in A. J., "and besides, you could probably pick up a couple of bucks for it if you sold it in town." Even as he said those words, he realized he shouldn't have, realized he didn't mean them. Selling the saddle might be the practical thing—something his father might do—but right then was no time to think about practical things.

"Got no need for a couple of bucks," snapped the old

man, "and it's damn sure I don't need that saddle for ridin'.
Not no more, I don't."

"I didn't really mean that, about selling the saddle," said
A. J., but he wasn't sure whether Mr. Tubbs even heard
him.

"Fool idea I had in my head," the old man said thoughtfully. "Why, I figured comin' up here to the place, I'd talk
with them new owners and supposed maybe, just maybe,
they'd sign me on to ride for 'em." He laughed a peculiar
laugh that sent a chill up A. J.'s back.

"Oh, no heavy work—nothin' like that, mind you. But
since I'd been around here on the place so many years and
knowed all there is to know about it, well, I figured there'd
be plenty of things I could tell 'em that would be a help. I
could show 'em where the good water is and some short
cuts up to them mountain meadows . . ." He let the
thought die and stood silently for a few moments, the saddle
at his feet. Then he shrugged.

"But these people here—" and he gestured across the
valley at the housing project "—sure as hell, they don't
need no cowboys to ride for 'em. 'Specially not no foolish
ol' critter the likes of me. 'Sides, they got 'em that there
dude in the purple shirt with orange flowers on it, and them
too-tight boots." He laughed again, then stooped and lifted
the saddle by its pommel.

"Let me help you," said A. J., stepping forward.

The old man waved him away. "I can manage, sonny,"
he said. "All my life I been carryin' saddles and never yet
needed no help."

Turning, he walked away from the road, and struggling
with the weight of the saddle, made his way to where the
grass was higher than his knees. Eloise sniffed and brushed
at her eyes with the back of a hand, and A. J. climbed into
the car to wait. Settling down he swallowed hard, then

looked around him. One thing's sure, he thought, there's a lot more room back here without a saddle than there is with one. He sneezed, though, remembering the smell of it, and strange as it seemed, he realized he missed the saddle.

"With all that room back there you'll be needing company," the girl said. She handed A. J. the leash and urged Gwendolyn to jump up onto the back seat with the boy. A. J. sighed. Spence got into the car and started the engine.

Both of them watched the old man as gently, he put the saddle on the ground, looked down at it for a time, then straightened his back and turned toward the car. He walked stiffly, slowly, and A. J. thought he looked suddenly older, much older than even a hundred. More like *two* hundred. As he came closer, A. J. closed his eye and studied the old man through his contact. Tears coursed down Mr. Tubbs's cheeks, and as he bent to get into the Volkswagen, he was singing the words of that mournful song he had been humming earlier.

> *Show me the yearlin' to rope and to brand.*
> *Out where the sagebrush is dusty and gray*
> *Make me a cowboy again for a day.*

When Mr. Tubbs was settled in his seat and had pulled the door shut, he folded his hands in his lap and Spence shifted into first and slowly headed back toward the highway.

The dude in the purple shirt with orange roses on it waved as they passed the sales office.

"Y'all come back, hear?" he called after them.

15

Nobody had much to say during the first few miles on the drive back to town. Eloise sniffled a few times and then she said, "This is awfully pretty country, Mr. Tubbs. I can see why you like it so much."

"Yup," he answered, nodding, but it wasn't as if he had really heard what she said. Then he was humming again. It was that same song, and before long A. J. found himself humming with the old man. Just a bar here and there; it was a haunting tune. The boy looked down beside him at the dog. Gwendolyn wasn't as big as the saddle; at least she didn't take up as much room, even though she was resting

her head on his leg. She smelled as bad as the saddle though, but in a different way. It wasn't a sneezy kind of smell. Curled up like a snail, Gwendolyn was sleeping and she was snoring. One good thing you could say for that saddle—at least it didn't snore.

"If you please, missy," said Mr. Tubbs, "I'm afraid I hear the call of nature. I'm right sorry."

Up ahead was a side road that cut through a stand of trees. "I'll drive on up there," said Spence, "so you can have some privacy." She slowed the car and made the turn into the side road. The old man climbed out and walked off several yards to some bushes. Turning sideways, Eloise placed her arm on the back of the seat and faced the boy.

"You were right, A. J.," she said softly. "This was a foolish thing for us to do. It turned out all wrong."

"You didn't know it was going to work out this way when you had the idea. You had no way of knowing what they'd done to the old man's ranch."

"I know," she said, "but I should have used my head. I mean, that poor man is *so* old—anything could've happened to him on this trip."

"Nothing did, so forget it."

"We're still not home yet."

"Yeah," said the boy, "but we're almost ready to head home. If I remember right, it's downhill almost all the way from Flagstaff. We can get back to town, see the old man's friend, grab something to eat, and coast all the way home to Tucson."

"Maybe seeing his friend will cheer him up," the girl said.

"Maybe."

Then Mr. Tubbs was back in the car and the boy settled down in his seat and Gwendolyn stirred. She looked up at him with her sad brown eyes, her tail wagging, thumping

against the serape on the back seat. She shifted her wrinkled head on his lap, then dropped off to sleep again. Within two minutes she was snoring—more a wheeze, actually—again.

"I think this dog has sleeping sickness, or something," A. J. said. "All she does is sleep."

"Bassets are that way," the girl told him. "If they aren't sniffing or wagging their tails, they're sleeping."

"Soft life," said A. J. "My mother's poodle doesn't sleep that much."

"Maybe she has insomnia."

"Who? My mother or her dog?"

Spence and A. J. laughed, though there wasn't much humor in it. Nobody spoke again until they were back in Flagstaff.

"Do you know how to get there?" Eloise asked Mr. Tubbs.

"Get where?" asked the old man.

"To where your friend lives," said the girl. A. J. thought he detected a note of impatience in her voice.

"Yup," said Mr. Tubbs. "Once I been to a place I can always find it again. Just head straight and we'll pick up the highway that leads up to the Grand Canyon. We'll go north, then. The home where my friend lives—it's maybe two, three miles out of town."

As they drove through Flagstaff the old man gave directions. They passed a large shopping center and the road zigged then, and they seemed to be getting into a more rural area. For several more minutes they followed the road.

"Up yonder on the right," the old man said, leaning forward in his seat. "Up in that stand of tall pines, beyond the split-rail fence."

After passing a school they turned right onto a driveway

that led to a parking area in front of an old but well-kept two-story building of pale tan rock.

"Peculiar," said the old man. "Used to be they had rocking chairs on the front porch. Last time I visited ol' Arnie, me'n him, we sat and rocked and talked away the whole of an afternoon. That Arnie—always was one for chewin' the fat."

They stood beside the car for a few moments, looking at the old building. "I don't see any old people around," said A. J.

"I hope we didn't miss visiting hours," said Spence. Then the three climbed the slight rise that led to the county home and mounted the gray-painted wooden steps of the front porch. Beside the front door was a sign and A. J. squinted to read it: PIONEERS' HISTORICAL MUSEUM.

No words came when A. J. opened his mouth to speak.

"That sign . . ." said Spence, "this is a *museum!*"

"Danged if it don't say so!" said the old man.

"We're lost," said A. J., who had finally found his voice.

"But this is *it*," insisted the old man. "This is the home where I visited ol' Arnie. Right here we sat, right here on this very porch, and we talked and we rocked."

"When was that?"

Frowning, Mr. Tubbs nibbled at his lip in deep thought. "Seems like maybe a week ago, I remember it so clear. But no, it must've been in the summer of nineteen and thirty-one. Thirty-two, maybe."

A. J. slowly shook his head. "Nineteen and thirty-one!" he repeated.

"Yup, that was it, all right," Mr. Tubbs said brightly. "Nineteen and thirty-one for sure. That was the year ol' Cupcake broke her leg and we had to shoot her. Downright

shame. She was as fine a mare as ever carried a saddle.''

"But that's—that's almost half a century ago!"

"Time do fly, don't it, sonny?" said Mr. Tubbs.

"Yeah," said A. J. "It sure do. Well, let's at least go inside and see what we can find out about the home. Maybe they've just moved it to a different place.''

Opening the door, they stepped into a small hallway and were greeted by a slim, red-haired young man who was seated at a desk. Smiling, he looked up as they entered.

"Good afternoon," he said. "Here are some brochures for you and you're welcome to wander around and have a look at our displays. Everything is clearly labeled, but if you have any questions . . .''

"I've got a question," said A. J. "This place—was it ever an old people's home for the county?''

The redhead nodded. "It was the Coconino County Hospital for the Aged and Indigent," he said. "It opened in 1908 and operated until 1937, when it closed down. In 1961 it became a museum of the Northern Arizona Pioneers' Historical Society.''

"The indigent?" asked A. J. "That means this was what they called the county poor house?''

"Poor *farm,* actually," said the red-haired man. "They kept cows and pigs and chickens here and raised some vegetables—carrots, potatoes, beets, turnips, and that sort of thing.''

Shaking his head in disbelief, A. J. turned to the old man. "So this place you remember as being so great was the county *poor* farm!" he said. "And you thought you'd like to move in.''

"Mr. Tubbs came here once to visit a man he used to work with," Eloise explained. "That was back in 1931, he thinks.''

The redhead whistled. "Do you know his name?''

"Yup. Arnie Spack's his name."

"Let's have a look," the museum man said, and he led them into another room where there were display cases full of old medical instruments and equipment that looked as though they had been in use a hundred years before. Maybe even during the Civil War. Unlocking a case, he lifted from it a large old black-covered ledger. He opened it carefully and scanned its yellowed pages, the tip of his index finger running down line after line of tiny, faded handwriting.

"Here," he said eagerly, poking his finger midway down one page. "Here's your friend—Spack, Arnold Peter. He came to live here in 1928 and stayed until 1934 when he—well, when he passed away." He glanced up at Mr. Tubbs. "It was April 17, if that matters, sir," he added, and then, as if an afterthought, "Pneumonia."

"So now ol' Arnie's gone, too," Mr. Tubbs said quietly. He removed his Stetson.

"Gone *now?*" said A. J. "Gone *then* is more like it. Gone way back in nineteen thirty-four! Why, my father wasn't even born yet, and you make it sound like it was last week."

"But he just now found out," argued Spence, "when all along he'd been thinking Mr. Spack was alive."

"Ol' Arnie was older'n me by some years. Fact, he was gettin' on when I signed to ride for Mr. Pfeffer. Sort of showed me the ropes, Arnie did. Presently he left the ranch and come to live with a sister here in Flagstaff. When she up an' died on him wasn't no place for him to go but here. Just that once, I was able to get down here to visit the poor ol' fella. Wanted to come visit him again, but there was always somethin' else to be doin' an' I kept puttin' it off. Wish I'd made it oftener." He stared wistfully through a front window that looked out on the tall pines in front of the home. "Somehow I just figured he'd still be livin' here."

Carefully the red-haired man replaced the ledger book in the display case and locked it. "If you visited this place while it was operating, you might like to have a look upstairs," he said to Mr. Tubbs. "That's where all the bedrooms were. All of the rooms are used for museum displays now, except one, and that one is furnished as the rooms were when this was the poor farm."

Eloise thanked the attendant and he settled back at his desk as the three climbed the wide stairs to the second floor. The room the redhead had mentioned was a front room and it wasn't many steps from the stairway.

A. J. and Eloise followed the old man into the tiny cubicle and there was barely room for all three inside it. The walls were painted a dark gray, the color of clouds on a stormy afternoon, and from the high ceiling hung a single bare light bulb. Narrow and tall, the window had a dark green pull-down shade, and the floor was a patterned linoleum of dark green with bits of yellow and white in it. The high bed was white enameled iron, not much wider than a cot, and was covered with an old patchwork quilt. Beneath the bed were a chamber pot and a cuspidor. In one corner of the room was a tiny sink with two spigots, and beside the basin was a wash stand. There was a trunk at the foot of the bed, and in the corner, behind the trunk, was a radiator. The three stood quietly in the crowded cubicle.

It was a depressing room and A. J. didn't like it. The whole place was depressing, and he thought about how awful it must've been to live in a home like that. It gave him a crawly feeling, and he was glad his grandfather and Mr. Tubbs lived in the rest home back in Tucson instead of here. It smelled old and dusty now, the way museums usually smell, but he could imagine how it must've been back when it was the old people's home and the smells were of urine and cooking and disinfectants. Just thinking of it, he almost

gagged. Maybe Mrs. Koplin had been lucky, living and dying in her own home, and not in a place like this.

"Come on," said A. J., "let's get out of here. This place gives me the creeps."

"You said that about the rest home in Tucson, too," Spence reminded him. "It gave you the creeps, too."

"I know, but that rest home—it's paradise, compared to this."

"You're right," said Spence. "It must've been awful for the people who had to live here because there was no place else for them."

As they talked, Mr. Tubbs had been standing quietly in the doorway, looking into the room. Suddenly then he chuckled and stepped to the high bed and sat on its edge.

A. J. and Eloise looked at one another, then the girl asked, "What's funny, Mr. Tubbs?"

"Ol' Arnie Spack— *he* was funny," said the old man. "I recall a time when the whole lot of us went to a dance in a two-room schoolhouse in a little settlement not too far out beyond the Pfeffer place. A nice dance it was, an' lots of ranch families there. Well, a good many of the folks brung their little babies to the dance with them, an' left them in their baby baskets in the off room of the school while they was dancin' in the main room."

Mr. Tubbs laughed again and slapped his Stetson against his knee. "I tell you—that Arnie, he was somethin'. Somebody had a jug out beneath a tree in front of the schoolhouse an' Arnie, well he spent a good part of the evenin' tippin' that jug, an' presently he pulled me'n Dutch away from the dancin' an' led us into the other room where all them little babies was sleepin'.

"The three of us started movin' them babies around from one basket into another, until there wasn't a single tyke sleepin' in the basket it belonged in. Time the dance was

over it was late an' the mas an' pas just come in an' grabbed
their baskets and headed off for home.

"I tell you, it must've been the better part of a month
before they got all them little babies switched back to their
rightful folks. If that weren't somethin' . . ."

Spence and A. J. laughed with the old man, and when the
laughter was done, the boy suggested they leave.

"You two young'uns go on down to the flivver," said Mr.
Tubbs. "I'll just set here a minute or two an' be down
directly."

The sun was low in the sky, and as they walked toward
the VW, A. J. shivered in the chill of late afternoon and
zipped his jacket. "I'm worried about him," said Eloise, "I
really am. Today has been full of disappointments for Mr.
Tubbs."

"The whole trip has," A. J. agreed. "First of all seeing
his marshal pal, Buck, who has to play pretend cowboy at
his age, and then seeing how the saloon in Prescott has
changed."

"And think of how he must've felt at the ranch today,"
said Spence. "I mean, seeing how they had chopped it up
and were making it into a cheapie subdivision. When he
left his saddle out there—honestly, A. J., I could hardly
keep from crying."

"Stopping here sure hasn't helped him much, either."

"I was wrong about us making this whole trip. It was
supposed to cheer him up," said the girl, "and my
God . . ."

"Yeah, I know—'Happy birthday, Mr. Tubbs.'"

"At least he seems to be taking it fairly well, though,"
said Eloise. "I mean, him telling us the funny story about
switching the babies. Maybe he is okay."

The boy didn't answer. He was looking toward the door
to the museum, watching for the old man, when the red-

haired attendant stepped outside, locked the front door, and started down the steps.

"Hey, wait!" A. J. called to him. The redhead stopped as A. J. and Spence hurried toward him.

"The old man—he's still inside!"

"I hope he's okay," said the girl. "He told us to go on ahead because he just wanted to stay behind a couple of minutes."

"Didn't realize he wasn't with you when you left," the man said apologetically. He fished in his pocket for a ring of keys, then climbed the front steps, the girl and boy following.

"We left him in the poor-farm room—he was sitting on the edge of the bed," explained A. J. as the attendant unlocked the door. We should have known better than to leave him alone like that, the boy thought. Feeling the way he must be feeling, no telling what's happened to him.

They went up the inside stairs two at a time to the second floor, where they found Mr. Tubbs stretched out on the bed, his Stetson resting on his chest, his eyes closed, his toothless mouth open. He was snoring. A. J. breathed a quiet sigh of relief.

Stepping to the side of the bed, Spence gently touched the old man's shoulder. "Mr. Tubbs," she said. "Mr. Tubbs—it's time for us to leave here. They're closing up."

The old cowboy opened his eyes, blinked a few times, and glanced about the room. He frowned, as if he wasn't sure where he was.

"Shoot," he said. "Don't know what come over me. Don't usually doze off like that." Slowly he sat up and swung his legs over the side of the bed. A. J. helped him to his feet. The red-haired man stood aside as the three went carefully down the stairs, A. J. and Spence walking on either side of the old cowboy. On the first floor the boy

nodded his thanks to the museum attendant and they stepped outside.

Mr. Tubbs seemed to be dazed, A. J. thought as they walked toward the car. Dazed, and less sure of his step. He was shuffling more than before, and it worried the boy.

For a few minutes they drove around Flagstaff looking for a place to eat. Not far from the Northern Arizona University campus, Spence found a pizza parlor and pulled into the parking lot. "How's pizza sound?" she asked enthusiastically.

"Sounds like a winner," A. J. said, leaning forward. He startled Gwendolyn, who yelped. "Oh, jeez, I keep forgetting this silly dog's in back with me. That saddle might've smelled, but at least it never barked at me. Sorry, pooch," he said, scratching her behind the ears. She made happy sounds and plopped a fat paw on his leg. He rearranged the dog so he could get out of the car. Inside the restaurant they found a table in the far corner. A. J. looked around and was pleased to see that most of the customers were college-age people, and not old folks, for once.

"What are we eatin'?" asked Mr. Tubbs.

"Pizza," said the girl.

"A piece o' what?"

"Pizza—that's what it's called," A. J. said. "P-i-z-z-a. Haven't you ever eaten any?"

The old man shook his head.

"You'll love it," Spence said.

"What's it like?"

"It's sort of like a pie, only it has tomato sauce and cheese and sausage or something else good on top of it."

Mr. Tubbs wrinkled his nose. "I like *apple* pie with cheese on it. Never ate no tomato pie."

"Just try the pizza," said the girl. "It's spicy—you'll love it."

"Does it take much chewin'? Don't have my teeth."

A. J. groaned softly. "Not much—you can probably gum it."

"An' what does a person drink in this place?" Mr. Tubbs wanted to know.

"How about cola?" asked A. J. "That's what I'm having."

The old man shook his head. "Can't have that—it's bad for my acme."

Eloise laughed. "You mean *acne*."

"Yup, it's bad for that, too, I reckon."

The girl smiled. "They have beer, Mr. Tubbs—how'd you like a beer?"

The old man's eyes brightened and he grinned, his tongue licking at his lips. "I reckon that'd be jus' fine."

When the waitress came to their table, A. J. ordered a large pepperoni pizza, one iced tea, a cola, and a schooner of beer.

Eyeing A. J. suspiciously, the woman said, "I'll have to see your age card."

"Oh, for cripe's sake, the beer's not for me—it's for the old man. Ask to see *his* age card!"

The waitress looked at Mr. Tubbs and snickered. "I'll take his word for it that he's of age," she said, and then she walked toward the kitchen. The service was slow and A. J. became fidgety.

"Relax," Eloise told him. "Pizza always takes a long time to fix."

"I'm just antsy to be on the road," he answered. "The sooner we get home, the better it'll suit me. We'll get in that little rattletrap and just head south—no stops."

"How about Gwendolyn and Mr. Tubbs? They'll have to ——"

"Okay, so we can stop for *that*, but nothing else. When

we leave here we'll pick up a sack of hamburgers, so we won't have to stop at any restaurants on the road. We can just eat cold hamburgers while we're riding, when we get hungry."

"You're a great planner, aren't you?" the girl said.

"One of us has to be or else we'll be forever getting home." And then he said the word again: "Home. You know what? I was going to call home from Prescott and I forgot. I'll go call now while we're waiting."

The pizza had been served when A. J. returned to the table. "Did your folks remember you?" asked Spence.

"Wow," the boy said, helping himself to a slice. "Did they ever. I kind of wish they hadn't. Sounds like I'm going to be grounded for six months." He took a bite of pizza, and chewing, added, "Maybe even until my twenty-first birthday."

"Oh, they couldn't be *that* upset," said the girl.

"Couldn't they? You don't know my folks. They're *that* upset! And at the rest home they're pretty upset, too. They figured out who snuck Mr. Tubbs out of there and from what my mother said, you'd better not show your face around there again. Not ever! You'd better find another place to be a volunteer." A. J. swallowed and looked at Eloise Spencer.

"And that's not all," he said quietly. "They don't know whether all the fuss and commotion we caused had anything to do with it or what, but poor Gramps—he's not doing very well. My mother says he's failed a lot, just since last night."

"I'm sorry, A. J.," said Spence. "Do you think he's missing Mr. Tubbs's being there and telling all his stories?"

The boy shrugged. "Who's to know? Why, the doctors don't even know whether Gramps is aware of what's going on around him, or not. My mother says it would be a blessing if he—well, you know, if he died."

For a while they ate without talking, then A. J. asked Mr. Tubbs how he liked the pizza. He said it was tolerable, then drained his beer and said he'd like another. A. J. glanced at Spence. She nodded. He signaled the waitress.

As Mr. Tubbs began drinking his second beer, Spence looked at A. J. and frowned. "Your chin," she told him.

"What about my chin?"

"That's where it's going to be."

With his fingertips, the boy explored his chin. "Where what's going to be?"

"Your next pimple. You told me you only get one pimple at a time and that the one on your nose was about gone, so you expected one on your cheek or your chin. Well, it's going to be on your chin. I can see where it's starting to get red."

A. J. Zander was annoyed. "Come on," he said, "let's finish up and hit the road."

Eloise asked the waitress for a large paper cup of water and she left the restaurant to give Gwendolyn a drink. Mr. Tubbs picked up the check and carried it to the cashier and unfolded one of his fifty-dollar bills for her.

"I'm sorry," said the cashier, "but I'm not allowed to take anything larger than a twenty. So many counterfeits floating around, you know."

A. J. groaned and reached for his wallet.

"No wonder you're so rich, Mr. Tubbs," he said as they left the pizza parlor. "I don't think you ever paid for anything in your life!"

The old man chuckled.

16

Stiff and sore, A. J. Zander IV awakened and looked at his watch. Even squinting through the contact, he couldn't make out the time. It was too dark. He yawned, stretched. For a while he sat in his corner of the rear seat of the Volks, suspended somewhere between sleep and wakefulness. The dog beside him stirred and he dropped a hand on her shoulder and scratched. His eyes burned, his body ached, his head was thick and fuzzy with sleep. He wasn't quite sure just where he was, nor was he even sure exactly *who* he was, for that matter. Running his fingertips through his hair, he brought his hands down then to massage his face, to rub the sleepiness from his eyes.

Then he looked outside, through the car windows, and he remembered. They had left the pizza place and stopped at a hamburger drive-in where they had bought a large sack of burgers and a few orders of french fries. Spence had fed two of the large burgers—hold the trimmings—to Gwendolyn, and then they had piled into the car for the long drive home.

Out of Flagstaff it was mostly downhill. The Interstate dropped steadily and at one point the old white Volkswagen reached a speed of fifty-three miles an hour. A. J. supposed it set some sort of a record, at least for that trip. It was dusk when they stepped out of the restaurant and by the time they left town it was full dark. The boy could just barely make out the silhouettes of the last of the tall trees as they passed from the big pine country and moved into the more barren, desert reaches of the lower elevations. It wasn't long before Spence lifted her foot from the accelerator and let the auto follow an exit ramp into a roadside rest area.

"What're we stopping for?" he asked.

"Tired," she said. "I've had so little sleep these last couple of days that I'm in some sort of a stupor."

"We'll never get home if we keep stopping," complained A. J.

"We'll *really* never get home if I *don't* stop and get a little sleep," she argued. "Just twenty minutes and I'll be all set."

The rest area was a large one, with room for two or three dozen autos to park, and for several trucks to pull up in the lanes marked for larger vehicles. When Spence had nosed the VW into a parking slot, A. J. climbed out of the auto and looked around. There were a few other cars parked beneath the floodlights, which were mounted on poles high overhead. There were two ramadas, or shelters, and beneath each were two picnic tables. At the center of the rest area was a small building of native rock, with restrooms for women on one side, men on the other. Not far from it was a

round tower made of the same kind of rocks. A. J. judged it to be twenty-five or thirty feet high, with a staircase that spiraled up around it to a viewing platform on its top. Beyond the restrooms, the tower, and the ramadas, the rocky ground dropped sharply, and the terrain below was rough, with shrubs and scrub trees everywhere, as far as his good eye could see in the pale light of the floods. It was nasty country.

When he had returned to the car, the girl already was asleep, and Mr. Tubbs pulled his seat forward so A. J. could climb into the back seat.

"Fetch me the bedroll, please, sonny," the old man said. A. J. pulled it out and handed it to Mr. Tubbs.

"Just hand it back when you're finished with it and I'll stash it away," said the boy.

"Nope," the old man replied. "I'll keep it—use it for a pillow."

Being careful not to disturb Gwendolyn, the boy settled back and quickly dropped off to sleep. How long he slept he didn't know. Later, when he came awake, it was pitch black and he sat numbly in the rear seat, remembering, finally, where and who he was, and he wanted to settle back and lose himself again in the comfortable sleep.

A thousand thoughts darted through his mind. He wondered how things were at home and he thought about Gramps. "Failing." The word bothered him. He was glad he had thought to call his folks from Flagstaff, so they wouldn't be as worried as surely they had been. He was anxious to get home, yet the reception he knew would be his made him dread that homecoming. He'd explain it all to them—the whole story—so they'd understand. I was drugged, he'd tell them, and carried off by that girl and her bandit accomplices and——. No. That wouldn't work. He'd already told them on the telephone where he was and

what he had done. He'd have to think of something else.
He'd manage, though; he always did. But for right now the
important thing was getting back to Tucson and getting Mr.
Tubbs back to the rest home. He'd had enough of the old
man to last him for a while. Of all old people, for that
matter. Except Gramps, of course. And then he remembered what Mr. Tubbs had said to Buck, the phony marshal.
"The kid's granddaddy is a friend of mine," he had said, or
something like that. He'd never really thought of it that
way—them being "friends." Just then, A. J. didn't know
what to think of Mr. Tubbs, so he decided not to think *anything* about him. He tried to put the old cowboy entirely out
of his mind.

But it didn't work, because just then he realized that the
old man wasn't in the front seat of the car. Off widdling
again, he supposed. Mr. Tubbs must've widdled at least
twenty gallons since they left the rest home. He looked at
Spence, whose head rested against the side window.

"You awake?" he asked. There was no reply.

"Spence!" he said more loudly. "You still sleeping?"
She didn't stir. A. J. leaned forward and shook her shoulder. "Eloise!" he said sharply.

The girl raised her head. "What?" she asked sleepily.

"You awake?" he asked, his voice softer now.

"No, I'm sound asleep."

"Maybe you should wake up so we can leave. I can't see
my watch, but we must've been here for hours. The sky is
black. Must be midnight or after, and you said twenty minutes. Some nap." Gwendolyn was snoring.

"I'm numb," she answered, "positively numb."

"We haven't had much sleep, last couple of days."

"When is this?" the girl asked groggily.

"What do you mean?"

"I mean, what day is it? What night?"

"If it's before midnight it's still Saturday, otherwise today is Sunday. It's all one big blur to me. It's been the longest Saturday of my life."

Sitting up, the girl stretched, then looked around. "Where's Mr. Tubbs?"

"Out getting fresh air, I suppose. He was gone when I woke up a couple of minutes ago."

"I'm hungry," Eloise said. "Why don't you pass me a hamburger."

"They're not back here," answered the boy. "They're up front on the floor by the old man, remember? We figured they'd be safer with him than with Gwendolyn."

The girl looked on the floor of the front seat. "They're not here," she said. "And neither are Mr. Tubbs's boots. They're gone, but his bedroom slippers are here. He told me once that he never wears the boots anymore unless he—A. J., I'm worried."

"What's to worry about? He's old enough to take care of himself. He's got his bedroll with him—probably he's stretched out sleeping somewhere on the ground. Cowboys always like to sleep on the ground."

"You're probably right," Spence said trying to sound cheerful. "But let's make sure. Let's have a look around for him."

"Okay," agreed A. J. "I'm ready for a stretch, anyway." So the boy climbed from the rear seat of the VW holding the dog's leash, but the basset didn't stir.

"C'mon, girl, wake up," Eloise called to the dog. Gwendolyn opened an eye. "Want to go outside?" The dog perked up, stood on the rear seat, shook herself and, wagging her tail, jumped from the auto.

It was chilly and an icy wind swept down out of the mountains and across the open country. Shivering, A. J. zippered his jacket. With Spence holding the basset's leash,

they started for the closer of the two shelters. A middle-
aged man and woman were at one of the tables under the
ramada. Each held a steaming coffee mug, and between
them was a large Thermos bottle.

"Excuse me," Eloise said, approaching their table. They
looked up at her. "Have you seen anything of an old man, a
real old man, around here?"

The man and woman exchanged glances, then both shook
their heads. "We only just got here," said the man.
"You're the first people we've seen."

"Well, if you happen to see him, tell him we're looking
for him, would you please? We're in that white Volks."

"Sure," the man said. "We'll tell him. Good luck."

The walked toward the other ramada then, circling
around the few trees and shrubs in the rest area. As they
passed the stone building, A. J. stepped inside to check the
men's room. It was empty. The floodlights overhead bathed
the entire rest area in an eerie, pale glow and cast long,
weird shadows. Bugs swarmed around each of the high
lights. There were maybe a half dozen autos and campers
pulled up in the area for cars, and two long semi-rigs were
stretched out in the truck parking lane. There was no one in
the other ramada, which was close to the edge of the rest
area. Not far beyond it the land began to drop sharply to the
rocky, tree-covered stretch below. A. J. saw that it was
darker down there than before.

"Now I'm really worried," said the girl. "I mean, where
could he have gone?"

"Let's climb the tower," said the boy. "Maybe we can
see him from up there." They hurried to the rock tower and
A. J. climbed the circling steps, two at a time. The girl
stayed below with the dog. With one eye closed, A. J. carefully studied the entire rest area, as best he could through
his single contact. It was useless. There was nothing to be

seen but the few cars and trucks, the ramadas, the restrooms, and plenty of dark shadows. Slowly he followed
the steps to the ground.

"Nothing," he said. "Maybe if we had a flashlight . . ."

"There's that one in the car," said Eloise.

They hurried to the VW where Spence reached beneath
the dashboard and produced the flashlight. She flicked the
switch.

"It's not the brightest I've ever seen," said A. J., "but
it'll help." He took the light and examined it.

"A. J.," said the girl sharply, "shine the light down
there, on Mr. Tubbs's seat." The boy reached past the girl
and aimed the beam where she had directed.

"His money belt!" said A. J. "I hadn't noticed it before.
It was too dark."

For a moment they stood silently, then Spence sucked in
her breath sharply. "Apaches!"

"Apaches—what?" asked the boy.

"Mr. Tubbs is gone and the bag of hamburgers is gone. I
mean, what you said about the Apache old people—how
they take some food and go off into the desert to die . . ."

To die! The words sent a chill down A. J. Zander's spine.
To die! And with his boots on, the way cowboys do!

"My God," the boy said softly. "You don't think——"
He paused. "That means that, if we don't find him, if he *has*
gone off like that, and if he dies out there, then I've as much
as killed him!"

Suddenly the boy's legs went weak and he felt as if someone had hit him in the belly with a balled-up fist. He leaned
against the car for support.

"My God, I didn't mean *any* thing——" The words stuck
in his throat. A. J. lowered himself onto the front seat of the
car, behind the steering wheel.

"No," he said, slowly shaking his head. "Nothing like

that. He wouldn't have just walked out there to—to die!"

And then A. J. was on his feet. "Put that money belt on under your jacket," he told Spence, "and then see if you can get some help. Maybe a highway patrol car'll come along, or something."

"What are you going to do, A. J.?"

"Look for him."

"But it's dark down there. You'll never find him, and there must be snakes. I'm sure it's crawling with snakes!"

"Spence, I've *got* to find him."

"In the morning, A. J."

"It's cold and the old man—he could die of exposure before morning. Isn't that what they call it? Exposure? And he must've been gone for a couple of hours, already. A guy that old should be careful of the cold night air."

"I'm sorry, A. J.," said the girl. "I'm sorry I got you into this."

"Oh, shut up. You didn't know anything would happen and neither did I." He sighed. "Old people," the boy muttered, and then he was on his feet.

With one eye closed, he stood beside the car, looking around, trying to decide which direction Mr. Tubbs might've taken. One guess was as good as another.

"I'll see you," he said, and then he started walking toward the far ramada. For a hundred feet or so, he walked quickly, and then A. J. Zander began to run.

"Be careful, A. J.!" he heard Spence call through the darkness. Already, she sounded very far away, as Randolph Scott disappeared in the night.

17

At the edge of the rest area he paused and flipped on the flashlight, playing its weak beam on the sharply dropping hillside below. It wasn't what you'd call a mountain or a cliff or anything dramatic like that, but A. J. dreaded the thought of making the descent to where the ground leveled off far below, especially in the darkness. He turned off the flashlight and stuck it in his hip pocket and cupped his hands around his mouth.

"Mr. Tubbs!" he called out, "Mr. Tubbs!" His voice carried far in the night. He paused for a moment, listening, then shouted again, "Answer if you hear me! I know you're

out there!'' The only other sound to break the silence was the hum of traffic on the Interstate.

Playing the flashlight's beam on the rocky hillside again, he quickly charted a course down the rough slope, then stepped cautiously over the edge. He'd use the light only occasionally, he decided, in order to save the precious beam. Carefully he picked his way, moving sideways, like a crab, or whatever creature it was that moved sideways, and leaning his weight back toward the slope, so that if he fell, he wouldn't tumble headlong into the treacherous darkness. A foothold gave way and he slid for some yards on the loose gravel before he was able to catch himself and regain balance. His heart was beating fast, less from the exertion than from the fear of the black unknown below, of falling, of what he'd find in those rugged, rolling low hills, or maybe of what he *wouldn't* find.

Moving slowly, he picked his way carefully. He flashed on the light and squinted through the contact and saw that he was within a dozen feet of the bottom. And after that? After that, he didn't know. A few steps further he lost his footing again, slipping, sliding, and he moved his feet quickly, scrambling as though running, to catch himself, and that carried A. J. the last several feet down the hill.

Shining his light on the ground around him, the boy picked up a rock about the size of a softball and he hefted it in his hand. ''In case of a snake,'' he said aloud, and the back of his neck prickled at the sound of his own voice. For a few moments he stood at the bottom of the hill, panting to regain his breath, and finally he moved out.

It was difficult walking. The rock-strewn earth was uncertain underfoot and with the low, rolling hills, there was no way of maintaining a steady pace. The branches of the trees seemed to reach out to whip at him, to snag his clothing. He didn't know what kind they were. Scrub oak,

maybe. Or juniper. Not that it mattered. They were gnarled and twisted and in the pale light of the occasionally switched-on flashlight, they took on grotesque shapes.

"Mr. Tubbs!" he shouted over and over again. "Answer me, Mr. Tubbs!" but his cries brought no response. Picking his way carefully, he imagined a snake coiled beneath each footfall.

"Where *are* you, old man!?" It was more a command than a question. A. J. laughed to himself. Here he is, yelling his lungs out, and the old man probably wouldn't be able to hear him, anyway, unless he was awfully close, being as "deef" as he was.

Now it was colder, and coming down the hill the boy had begun to perspire, and the cold bit at the moisture beneath his windbreaker. He felt miserable.

What am I doing here? he asked himself, but he had no answer. He didn't know *what* he was doing there. He was cold and he was sweaty, there were snakes and probably mountain lions and bears out there—maybe even crocodiles, for all he knew—and there he was, risking his life for a silly old man who really meant nothing to him. Gramps' friend.

But it was his fault that Mr. Tubbs was out there, that the old man had wandered off by himself, and so A. J. had no other choice, he realized, than to be the one who went looking for him. In his mind he tried to juggle it so that someone else would be to blame, would be the one to look for the old man, but he couldn't. It landed squarely on his own shoulders. If he had his druthers, he'd druther be in bed, or watching an old movie on TV. Again he laughed, this time out loud. "Druthers." That's the kind of word the old man used. Cripes, he thought, the old cowboy was rubbing off on him.

Stopping, he hollered out again and then called one more

time. It wasn't like an echo, yet he could hear his own voice carrying far into the distance, where it was swallowed, in time, by the darkness.

High overhead was a fingernail slice of moon, and the sky was filled with stars. Looking up through his good eye, he saw what he supposed were more stars than he had ever seen at any one time in his life. It made him dizzy and light-headed and he squatted then, his head hung low between his knees, until he felt better. Then he stood and began moving again.

For what seemed like hours, he walked, searching, calling, probing occasionally into the darkness of the desert night with the flashlight's weak beam. Now, through the single contact, he could make out the darker shapes of trees around him, set against the softer darkness.

A. J. started jogging then, or maybe it was trotting, if there was a difference. He was chilled and he hoped the added movement might warm him. "Old man, old man, old man!" he cried out as he ran. A sharp branch reached out of the alien night and snagged the sleeve of his jacket and ripped it, but the boy ran on. Soon he was breathless and the pauses between his cries became longer as he gasped for air.

It was old Mrs. Koplin, all over again. Or was it? No, not at all, he thought. Back then, back when he was a kid, *that* was Mrs. Koplin. But now, tonight, it was Mr. Tubbs and this was A. J.'s fault. Mrs. Koplin and Mr. Tubbs had nothing to do with one another. They probably wouldn't even like each other, A. J. thought, and he laughed to himself and the shortness of his breath made him cough. This business now, with Mr. Tubbs, had nothing to do with Mrs. Koplin, he realized, and he pushed on through the desert underbrush, and he knew that more than anything else in the world, he wanted to find Mr. Tubbs, not because it was

his fault the old man was lost, but because he wanted to be
with him again. He *liked* him.

Topping a low hill, he ran faster on the downward slope
and as he neared the draw at its base, he stepped on a loose
pebble and his foot turned. His ankle twisted violently and
sharp pains daggered up his leg. He raised the injured leg,
wrapped his arms around it below the knee, and hopped on
the other foot, over the uneven ground. *"It hurts, it hurts!"*
he cried aloud, and then he sucked in his breath and fought
to keep the tears from building in his eyes. Placing the foot
gingerly on the ground, he tried to put weight on it, but the
throbbing pain increased. He had to keep going, though; he
had to move on in order to find the old man. This he knew.
Through his tears came a laugh. The phrase "had to keep
going" ran through his mind again and again, and the words
made him laugh, because they were cornball hero words,
the kind of words the good guy in the white hat would say in
a Western when the going got tough. The old man—*he*
might say something like that. Or might *have,* back when he
was a kid riding the range and chasing cows on that damned
ranch. Again he flicked on the light and flashed the beam
around. Trees, rocks, nothing else.

The pain in his ankle became more intense and now anger
was building within him. Lowering himself to his other
knee, he let his fingers gently probe the injured ankle and
the flesh around it felt soft and puffy and it hurt to touch. He
shined the light on the ankle and saw that it had swollen
quickly. A broken leg; that was all he needed. Or a sprained
ankle, maybe. That would be bad enough.

How far had he gone? A couple of miles, maybe. Easily
that. He looked in the direction he'd come from, but
couldn't even see the glow of the rest-area floodlights.
Maybe *more* than a couple of miles. Five? He had no way of
knowing. He wasn't good at judging time or distance or

direction. Why bother when there are watches and speedometers and compasses? Raising his wrist, he looked at his watch. It said two-eleven, but was it correct? It seemed later than that, much later. *Seemed*, but was it actually? He flashed the light around the ground and spotted a broken branch that would serve as a crutch, or at least a cane, and painfully he dragged himself toward it and picked it up.

The anger, the frustration, grew within him as the pain became greater, and he wanted to scream out in the night to let the world know that he, Alfred Jacob Zander IV, was angry. He was angry at the rock that had twisted his ankle and he was angry at the ankle itself, for twisting so easily and failing him just when he needed a strong ankle. And he was angry at Eloise Spencer for having gotten him into this whole thing and he was angry at the old man because he *was* the old man, because he had wandered off into the wilds the way the Apache old people used to do, but especially because he was old.

But mostly, A. J. was angry with himself. He was angry with himself for having treated the old man the way he had, and he realized that Spence had been right, that he hadn't liked the old man simply because he was old and made him think of Mrs. Koplin, and that was a stupid reason for not liking someone. She had been right about the fear, too, he realized now, and he was angry with himself about that, because he knew that he didn't like being around old people because they reminded him that some day he'd get old, too, and useless, and then he would die, and *that* was something he refused to think about. And for this, especially, A. J. was angry with himself.

He could even taste the anger in the salty tears that streamed down his cheek and into his mouth, and he wiped at them with his sleeve and pulled himself to his feet, and

using the branch to lean on, began walking again. Suddenly the branch snapped and A. J. lost his balance and sprawled to the ground.

"God *damn* it!" he cried out. "God *damn* it, answer if you hear me, old man! *Ans*wer!"

"Sonny?" came a thin voice through the night. "That you out there, sonny?"

"Where *are* you?" demanded A. J.

"Over here," the thin voice said. "Just you follow the sound of my talkin' . . ."

18

Pulling himself to his feet, A. J. limped painfully over the rough ground toward the sound of the old man's voice. "Just keep making noise," he hollered out. A. J. didn't even listen to the words the old man was saying. In fact, he wasn't even sure the old man was saying anything that made any sense. It was just a sound to follow in the night, like a radio beacon the old airplane pilots followed. With every step the pain raced up his leg.

As the voice became louder, fuller, A. J. flashed the light around, looking for the source of the sound. Then he spied the old man, sitting cross-legged beneath a distant tree. Closing his bad eye, he saw the old man clearly, seated on

the ground against the bedroll, comfortable as could be, eating a hamburger. Gumming it.

"You hurtin', sonny?" asked the old man.

"My leg," he said. "I think I broke it or maybe just sprained the ankle. God, but it hurts." He eased himself to the ground beside the old cowboy.

"Know what they do with horses that bust a leg, don't you?" asked Mr. Tubbs.

"Yeah, they shoot 'em. So if you've got that six-shooter in that bedroll of yours, old man, you might as well pull it out and fire away, for all I care. I'm really hurting."

"Lemme have a look."

A. J. was startled. "You mean for the gun?"

The cowboy laughed. "Nope, sonny," he said. "Lemme have a look at that leg of yours."

Scooting closer to the old man, he raised the leg and put it down slowly in front of him.

"This hurt?" Mr. Tubbs asked, and he began touching the boy's ankle. A. J. yelped.

"*Yes,* it hurts!"

"An' this?"

The boy sucked in breath through his clenched teeth. "Yeah!"

"Well, then she's a sprain, sonny. Reckon we ain't goin' to have to shoot you, after all. Sprain's plenty painful, make no mistake of that, but you'll recover." The old man poked a hand into his blanket roll and pulled out an old, dirty Ace bandage. There wasn't *anything* the old man didn't have in that bedroll of his.

"Now, this ain't goin' to make it all better by a damn sight," Mr. Tubbs said, "but it'll help some."

"Want my shoe off?"

"It'd be better, but you'll need it on for walkin', I reckon. I'll just wind the bandage over the shoe for now."

It hurt as the old man wrapped the elastic strip tightly

around the arch of the foot—shoe and all—and then wrapped upward, round and round, until the bandage was spelled out. Then he pinned it. "Feel any better?"

A. J. said it did. Not a whole lot, but some.

"Then you'd best be turnin' off that electric torch," Mr. Tubbs said. "You'll be needin' it when you head back."

"When *I* head back?" the boy asked. "When *we* head back is what you mean."

"Nope," said the old man. "Me? I'm stayin'."

"But you *can't* stay out here, Mr. Tubbs," A. J. argued. "You'll *die* out here!"

"I'll die if I go back, too," the old man said. And then he added, "Presently, leastways."

"But that's different."

"Trail might be different," said Mr. Tubbs, "but once I get there it's gonna be the same place."

"Sure," said the boy, "but why take the short trail? Me, I'd rather take the long trail—the very *longest* one."

"Sometimes a fella gets weary on the long trail, sonny," said the cowboy. "Take them old Apaches you was talkin' 'bout, for instance. Sure, they could've took the long road and lived a spell longer, but like you said, they'd lived up their lives and they weren't much use for a whole lot else."

"Oh, God, Mr. Tubbs, I don't know what made me talk about those old Apaches. I didn't mean anything by it. I'm sorry, honestly I am. I know it must have seemed like I was hinting to you that you were old and useless and that you should maybe go off somewhere and die, like the old Apaches did, but believe me, I didn't mean it that way. It was just talk, just stupid loudmouth talk."

"Didn't once enter my mind that you was hintin' or any such a thing, an' besides, I'd heard all that times past, 'bout them Apaches. Truth is, it set me to thinkin', sonny. I *am* useless. Ol' an' useless. Anymore, all there is for me to do is set around an' wait to die."

"But you're *not* useless—that's the thing."

"It's been a few years since I was up to sittin' a horse or doin' a job of work." The old man chuckled. "An' you know, sonny, I just been goin' along foolin' myself of late, figurin' maybe I could sign on again at that ranch. Shoot, foolish is what I been. Plain foolish.

"My eyes come full open the last few days, though, an' I come to realize I've done my ridin'. Them days is long past."

"That's why you left your saddle up there on the ranch?"

"Yup, sonny. Somebody'll come across it an' put it to proper use, the way a saddle should be used. Do plenty more good that way than bein' in the closet back to the home."

"But there are other things to do, other ways to be useful besides riding a horse."

"Most any cowboy will tell you, ain't no job worth doin', 'less you can do it from the back of a cowpony."

"That's a lot of crap! Look at the way you fixed that car. Why, we'd have really been in a bad spot if you hadn't been able to repair it. We'd probably still be stranded up there on that mountain. People—they just don't stop these days to help folks in trouble. That's what my dad says, at least."

"Help would've come, sonny. Always does when you need it bad enough."

"And those motorcyclists back there at Black Canyon City—you got us out of that scrape, too, Mr. Tubbs," said A. J. He shifted and the pain shot up through his leg. "No telling what would have happened to Spence—to the missy—if you hadn't pulled out that big gun of yours and scared them off."

"Shoot," the old man said quietly, and then he chuckled. And A. J. laughed, too, but to himself. It came suddenly to him that he was trying to convince the old man that he wasn't worthless—that he was needed, that there were

things for him to do—when all along it had been A. J. who hadn't believed that. Now he realized he had been wrong. If only he could get the old man to believe it now.

For a time neither spoke. A. J. broke the silence. "So you think you aren't good for anything anymore and so you wandered off out here to die, just like that."

"Yup."

"But aren't you afraid? Afraid to die, I mean?"

"Afraid? Nope, not so's I could notice, at least. Curious? A might edgy? Yup, edgy and curious I was. It ain't as if dyin' is somethin' I been lookin' forward to these many years. Lots of things I'd be doin', given my druthers, but sonny, in some things a man got no choice. Dyin's one of them. Day a scalawag baby breathes his first, he starts dyin'. Ain't nothin' gonna stop it."

"Mr. Tubbs," the boy said slowly, "I think *I'm* afraid. I mean, afraid of getting old and dying."

"Figured that."

"But I mean, I'm just barely sixteen. It's not like I'm ninety or a hundred or whatever it is you are. I'm sixteen and I'm afraid to die."

"I reckon ever'body gets to feelin' that way one time or another, sonny, but it passes. A man comes to know that dyin's just a part of livin' an' he accepts it. Shoot, you can't walk around all your life carryin' fear on your shoulders like it was a hundred-pound sack of feed settin' up there."

The old man coughed. The night air was cold and A. J. supposed he'd never been more uncomfortable in his life. He wanted to leave, to go back to Spence and the car, but somehow he couldn't bring himself to leave Mr. Tubbs.

"Lemme tell you about ol' Dutch," Mr. Tubbs said after a while.

"You already did," said A. J. "Wasn't he the cowboy you were with when you splashed all that blood on your arms and scared the dudes out of the saloon?"

"Same feller," the old man said, "but it ain't the same story." Mr. Tubbs sat silently in the darkness for a while and A. J. wondered whether he was thinking or had dozed off or what. Then he began speaking again.

"Four of us boys rode to the railroad one time to pick up a string of fine horses Mr. Pfeffer had bought over to New Mexico. It were me'n Dutch and a couple other fellas. We thought we'd have an easy time of it, but turned out we didn't. Them horses, they'd been on the train a couple of days and they weren't feelin' their best.

"Well, comin' back down the weather turned bad. Terrible storm, it was, and while passin' through a narrow place, well, lightnin' struck close by and spooked them horses somethin' awful. They stampeded an' Dutch, he got throwed and trampled to beat hell. Them other riders went after Mr. Pfeffer's horses an' me, I stayed with ol' Dutch. He was so bad hurt I couldn't move him an inch from where he fell. Well, Dutch—he was a couple hours dyin', an' me, I merely sat there with him, doin' what I could an' that was precious little."

"Was he awake all that time?" the boy asked.

"Yup," the old man answered. "He just lay there, all battered and bloodied up an' all I could do was watch as the life run out of him like thick molasses comin' slow out of a spilled jug."

"Did he know?" A. J. asked. "I mean that he was dying?"

"'Course he knowed it, an' knowin' hurt him plenty, 'cause if ever a fella loved livin', it were Dutch. Always laughin', full of fun. So he fought dyin', fought it ever' inch of the way, an' he went out hard. Like a baby, he cried, an' he kept it up most of them two hours. Oh, he was afraid, terrible afraid. 'Don't let me die!' he cried, over an' over. 'Don't let me die!' As if there was anything I or anybody else could do to keep that from happenin'."

The old man was quiet again. Thinking, A. J. supposed. Remembering things that far back must be hard. Then he spoke some more.

"Dutch was as good a friend as ever I had. A good ol' boy to ride with. Toward the end I put my arms around his shoulders an' held him like he was a baby, thinkin' that might ease things for him, only it didn't. He just kept up that awful cryin', an' then it stopped.

"At that very moment I knowed he was gone, but still I kep' holdin' him an' rockin' him in my arms, an' I told myself right there that it'd be different with me. I figured whenever the time come, I wouldn't fight it, I wouldn't be afraid. Dutch bein' afraid—his tears an' cryin'—they didn't save him."

"How old was he?"

"Happened in the spring of the year, an' come that October, he'd 've celebrated his twenty-first birthday."

" 'Course, we buried Dutch right there, best we could, an' piled rocks over him to keep the critters away, an' one of the other boys—older fella—he said some words over him an' then we rode on with them horses."

A. J. could hear Mr. Tubbs shifting in his place. Then the old man was talking again.

"All of Dutch's belongin's we turned over to Mr. Pfeffer, 'cept I kept his dollar watch. It was battered an' broke up when he went under them horses—no good for keepin' time of day—but I put it in my pocket an' I've carried it to this day. Crystal was busted and the hands stopped the minute it happened. Well, I kept it in my pocket all these years, an' any time I got to fearin', I'd stick my hand in there an' feel of Dutch's watch an' that would help. I'd remember how Dutch had went, an' how bein' afraid made it harder for him, an' how it wasn't goin' to be that way with me. Shine your light over here, sonny."

The boy snapped on the flashlight and let its pale beam

fall on Mr. Tubbs's hand. A. J. closed one eye and looked closely at the watch with the smashed face, which lay in the old man's palm. Its hands were stopped at eleven-seventeen—the moment Dutch was trampled. The old man squeezed his fingers tightly around the watch, then opened his hand and extended it toward the boy.

"Here, sonny," the cowboy said. "You take this. Me, I've long ago run out of needin' it."

A. J. took the watch in his hand. It was still warm from Mr. Tubbs's pocket, Mr. Tubbs's hand. Now he looked more closely at its battered case, its broken face. Eleven-seventeen. A. J. shuddered. "No, I can't take this——"

"Keep it, sonny. Maybe it'll help you the way it's helped me. An' then, come the time you don't need it no more, just give it to somebody who does need it, an' tell 'im about poor ol' Dutch."

A. J.'s fingers closed around the watch for a moment, then he slipped it into a pocket. He didn't talk for a while. He sat on the cold ground, listening to Mr. Tubbs's heavy breathing and thinking about Dutch and the watch and about eleven-seventeen of one long-ago morning. Finally he spoke.

"You're sure?" he asked. "I mean about not going back with me?"

Mr. Tubbs sighed. "Yup, sonny, I'm sure. Mind's made up."

"Gramps—he's going to miss you. Mom said he's failing. I'll bet he misses you already, Mr. Tubbs. You and your stories."

"Poor ol' fella. He'll manage."

"Then I guess I'd better be getting back to the car. Spence is awful worried about you." A. J. stood carefully, trying to keep as much weight as possible on his good foot. He limped the short step or two to where the old cowboy

sat, turned on the flashlight, and leaned over to shake hands with him.

A. J. closed one eye and looked at the old man through the contact lens. There was a tear on Mr. Tubbs's cheek. They clasped hands then, and A. J. took one step backward. He could feel the tears building in his own eyes. He swallowed hard.

"You're not afraid?" he asked the old man.

"Nope," said the cowboy quietly. "I ain't afraid. You afraid?"

A. J. shook his head. "I don't know. Not for sure, at least," he said, then paused. "No, I don't guess I am." He moved back a few more steps, favoring the hurt leg. "Good-bye, Mr. Tubbs," he said, and then he turned the flashlight off and started limping into the darkness.

"Good-bye, sonny," the old man said. "An' tell the missy I thank her for what she done."

The pain was sharp and with every step A. J. wanted to cry out. The tears were flowing now, and his nose was full, and he felt as though a fist had been jammed down his throat. He sobbed, then sniffed and wiped at his face with a sleeve.

"Hold on, sonny!"

A. J. halted, turned, flipped on the flashlight. Mr. Tubbs was coming after him, the bedroll tucked beneath an arm.

"Now just where do you suppose you're goin'?" the old man called sharply.

"Back to the car."

"You ain't never goin' to make it that way," said the other. "Just look at them stars. Shoot, you're headed in the absolute wrong direction."

He pointed to the sky then, but A. J. had no idea what he was pointing at. "Lookie there," said Mr. Tubbs, "take your bearin's on that far bright one an' you'll be all set.

Shoot, you with a game leg headin' off goodness knows where, why, they'd *never* find you. Reckon I've just got to get you back to missy Eloise, else she's never goin' to see you again.''

They turned sharply in a different direction and the old man moved in close beside A. J.

"Lay your arm across my shoulder, sonny," he said. "That'll take some weight off that game leg of yours."

A. J. placed his arm on the old man's shoulder and the walking was easier and there was less pain in the leg. That hazy, gray image that for so long had been at the edge of his mind drifted forward, and for a split second he thought about Mrs. Koplin again. But then as quickly as the thought had come, it disappeared.

A. J. laughed.

"What's ticklin' you, boy?" asked the old man.

"You," he said. "You're tickling me. Not five minutes ago you were telling me about how useless you were, and now, here you are, rescuing me, instead of me rescuing you."

The old man chuckled again.

A. J. slipped his free hand into his pocket and the tips of his fingers touched the watch and he knew then that he wasn't afraid. It wouldn't be eleven-seventeen for a long time.

"Backward, turn backward, O Time, with your wheels," sang Mr. Tubbs as they walked through the darkness, and then Alfred Jacob Zander IV joined in singing.

Where the boy didn't remember the words, he just hummed.